A
Harlequin
Romance

PAPER HALO

PAPER HALO

by

KATE NORWAY

HARLEQUIN BOOKS
Toronto • Canada   New York • New York

PAPER HALO

First published in 1970 by Mills & Boon Limited,
17 - 19 Foley Street, London, England

Harlequin Canadian edition published July, 1971
Harlequin U.S. edition published October, 1971

Standard Book Number: 373-51505-7.

Printed in Canada

CHAPTER 1

OCTOBER was a beautiful month. Gossiping outpatients told one another daily that it was 'a regular Indian summer', and in the wards September's extra blankets were discarded. The earth, tucked up for winter, woke and stretched and smiled again. Funny, clean little wagtails came bobbing and dipping on the scrappy grass and the laundry cat sprawled in the morning haze too warm and idle to stalk them. Sun-yellow leaves, bleached to complement slate-grey skies, blazed theatrically against unforeseen blue. The farewell maple planted on the doctors' lawn by a Canadian SMO poked blood-red fingers into the soft air; the Nurses' Home was hung with tiny crimson pennons, and the beeches screening the labs burned tangerine in the late sun. It was so beautiful that nothing should have changed, nothing should have gone wrong. Perhaps we expected too much.

On the first day of the month Miss Tetlow took off her cap for good. She put on a strange brown fur-felt bucket with a pheasant's feather, climbed into her loaded Fiat and chugged off to a Merioneth cottage. Somewhere in the clutter she carried an inscribed salver from the students and a portable TV set from the sisters and staff nurses. The consultants had given her a cheque; the residents whipped round to pay for her photograph, which was to join its nine predecessors in the board-room. That was the end of her working life. It was the end of something for all of us at St. Finbar's.

'The old place won't be the same with a new matron,' Torfy Bates said that evening as we brooded in her bedroom. 'My bones say she'll be brisk and modern. And Fin's isn't that kind of hospital! Miss Tetlow kept it nice and trad, and that's the way it should be. Dignified, if not quite with it ... We've grumbled enough about the old faggot at times, but we're going to miss her, you know.'

I agreed. People have this stereotype image of a hospital matron: they take it for granted that anyone who stays in the profession long enough to land a top job becomes either an embittered martinet or a stone-faced recluse—and that if she's single she automatically gnaws her nails in frustration and takes it out on everyone within range. It isn't true: the old-time grouches don't get short-listed any more; they find themselves accepting smaller, scruffier hospitals, and the bright girls rise past them. So do the natural-born saints, and Miss Tetlow was one of those. 'You can say that again,' I said. 'She was old, and a bit shy really. Oh, she could lose her cool when people really deserved it, but I've never known her unfair. She fell over backwards.'

Torfy hugged her long skinny legs and blinked at me through her elf-pointed glasses. 'This Macintosh woman'll be new-brooming around, wrecking everything, if she's anything like what the tutors are saying.'

'What *are* they saying?' They had their channels, and they were probably right.

'Oh, they've been doing their homework. At least, Miss Jebb has. Apparently she's got a rep for taking over run-down businesses, as it were, building them up, and then clearing off to reorganise somebody else. A sort of NHS hatchet-woman. She never stays longer than two years in any Admin job.'

That sounded feverishly rootless. Miss Tetlow had been at St. Finbar's for more than twenty years. 'Then let's hope she confines her itchy fingers to improving the buildings—heaven knows they're shabby enough, bless 'em—and leaves us alone,' I said. 'Lord, we shall soon know. She'll be here tonight. Stand by for the revolution.'

That was on Wednesday. By Friday Miss Macintosh had shown the flag in every ward and department in the place. We had all seen her. We should all know her again. We were all faintly relieved.

When she appeared in Casualty with Mr. Sandbach, the Deputy, glooming alongside, I was filling in an admission slip for the Casualty Officer to sign: all I saw as I straightened up was a vertical little back in grey terylene and a pretty *broderie anglaise* cap perched above a pleat of well-brushed dark hair. But Sister Lamont met her head-on and told us about it afterwards. 'Very quick,' she said appreciatively. 'The bright eyes of a reforr-mer, I'm thinking, but she laughs a deal. Be thankful for small maircies. She's lovely eyes, I'll grant her that. Forty if she's a day, and still attractive. Och, it's the kind to watch: they can talk committees into anything!'

She had a point there. On Monday we were told that in future we'd be wearing disposable caps and collars, using disposable dressing towels, draw-sheets and barrier gowns, and giving injections with throw-away syringes. Within a week they were issued. Either Miss Macintosh moved fast or she had a galvanising effect on those who could. We began to worry about our uniform—we were proud of the lilac gingham that had always been a St. Finbar's speciality—and Torfy said that if Miss Macintosh thought people could feel like nurses in white overalls, or, worse, in disposable ward gowns, she would have a student revolt on her hands.

The next innovation affected only those of us who worked in Casualty and Outpatients. Sister called all the seniors into her office when she returned from a mystery trip to the office on Thursday morning. 'I've to see how you all feel about this,' she said. She paused to poke back a strand of brindled hair with the end of her pen. Somehow Sister Lamont always has a pen in her hand and this hair-poking is her most definitive gesture. I had seen her do it hundreds of times—talking to patients, arguing with housemen, taking nurses to task—and I knew that she did it when she was doubtful and when she was trying very hard to be fair. 'If ye're not in agreement, I doubt it'll go through ... Miss Macintosh is wanting us to try an interr-nal night duty rota. Just in the deparr-tment; not in the wards.' She looked at Torfy and me, and then at Sally Dane and Luke Martin, the third-years. 'Failing any staff nurse volunteering it'll not necessarily affect anyone but you four.

9

She doesn't want second-years left in charge down here at night and I'm of the same mind myself. Nurse Bates and Nurse Kennedy—you'll not be able to claim staff nurses' immunity until your certificates actually come through. How do you feel about it?'

'But why, Sister?' I wanted to know. 'Are we guinea-pigs for ward schemes? And is it so that we spend less time on nights? If it's to be for short periods, won't it be disrupting?' I could see Luke Martin nodding at my elbow, wanting to say the same.

'Not guinea-pigs,' Sister said. 'Matron feels that a three-monthly change system is fine for the wards, where they're always busy. But down here, where it's often slack after midnight, it's virr-tually solitary confinement. She thinks a week enough.'

Luke stuck out his bottom lip. 'You mean we'd be on one week in four? Doesn't give you much time to adjust, does it, Sister?'

'One in five, Mr. Martin. Since we'll be cutting out a pairrmanent night nurse I'm offered a part-time SRN who's asked for an occasional week of nights. Anyone else any objections?'

Staff Weaver, who is a pleasant but calculating redhead with an eye to the main chance, said: 'One thing will be an advantage if it's done internally, Sister. Presumably Night Super won't have any say in the rota? So if anyone wants to swop for personal reasons she'll have you to deal with and not Sister Duffy.'

Cathy Weaver knew perfectly well that Sister Lamont and Sister Duffy had been in a state of armed neutrality for years, ever since a first-year junior had been optimistically sent to take charge of Casualty at night. She had managed to burn out the Minor Ops steriliser, break Sister Lamont's treasured Coalport teapot and send seven casualties home without obtaining their names and addresses for the book. Since then only seniors had been allowed down there at night, and obviously Sister Lamont would be delighted to get the night-duty reins into her own hands. She gave Cathy one of her long cool

10

looks, pushed back her hair again and turned to me. 'Yes, Nurse?'

I capitulated. 'It *may* be a good idea, Sister. I've no objection until we've tried it.'

Torfy is not only taller, darker, older, quicker and livelier than I am, she is also much more forthright. It comes, perhaps, of having a row of older brothers. She said straight out: 'Look, do *you* want it, Sister? If you do, we'll muck in, of course. But if you *don't*, we'll kick up all hell to stop it.'

'Wheesht!' Sister folded away her smile. 'That's no way to talk, Nurse Bates. I think perhaps we should give it a wee whirr-l before we do any kicking up!'

Behind me the caramel voice of Randall Brown said: 'You could make it one week in six, Sister. I wouldn't mind nights from time to time.' He meant, of course, that the extra pay would be useful, because he has a jolly little wife and two shiny brown babies. For those of us who were not yet staff nurses there would be no extras and no option, but as far as I was concerned night-duty was its own bonus. I had always preferred the small intimate night world to the bustle and publicity of days. 'If that would suit you, Sister,' he added.

She looked pleased. 'The more the merrier. Fine. That will make it easier for everyone ... Eh, you're the mathematical one, Nurse Bates. When you've finished in the plaster room you can help me to work out the new timetable. The rota begins on Saturday, if we agree, so if any of you have existing arrangements you'd best let me have a chit before eleven ... All right, everybody. Get on. There are about five thousand patients out there in the hall, and every one with a bus to catch, by the sound of it.'

Torfy would be nettled, I knew, by being called 'the mathematical one'. Once, in her first year, Sister Russell in the private wing had queried a dilution she had made—and made correctly—and she'd said: 'Yes, I *am* sure, Sister. I do have A-level maths, you know!' That had not gone down very well, because Sister Russell is incapable of going through any arithmetical process whatever without using her fingers, matches and even teaspoons to count with. She is nevertheless

11

a kindly and capable woman, and a perfectly competent nurse provided she has someone else to add up for her. Evidently the incident was mentioned in the sisters' sitting-room, because every ward sister Torfy had worked for since had landed her with every calculation in the business, from working out dosages to fiddling the stock, with meaning little digs about her mathematical flair. 'Why can't I keep my big mouth shut?' she had said at the time. 'Look at you, Clare. You never get lumbered with things like that. And it isn't because you haven't got the brains—any moron can do medical maths—it's because you don't stick your neck out. I've a jolly good mind to spread the dark secret of that poetry prize you had—then they'll make you do all the lyrics for the Christmas concert.'

The Brooke Memorial Prize was the only one I had to show for my last year at school—but Torfy had walked off with half a dozen. She looks clever too, with her bony face and blue-black fringe, and her uncontrollable limbs. Yet she is infinitely more popular with the men than any of the really pretty girls in our set. Not that doctors ever do show much inclination to cultivate dumb beauty: they are fully alive to the advantages of sorting out the right helpmeet whether they see her as an SRN—'jolly useful in general practice, old man'—or as the only daughter of a wealthy consultant who is due to retire in the foreseeable future. I doubt very much whether David Leckie would ever have displayed any interest in me if he hadn't happened to be my father's houseman and one of his former students.

I was thinking about David as I ploughed through my share of the morning's dressings. There was a long queue out in the big hall—we had long ago abandoned the appointments system except for afternoon outpatients—but with four or five of us in the dressings section it would reduce to a trickle by lunchtime. Until Torfy joined me I had only Eira Hughes, a scatty little second-year, to help me at the big centre table, and Cathy Weaver and Johnny Winter were hard at it in the end cubicles. There were two other staff nurses, but Frances Hill was on holiday and Randall Brown was running the ENT clinic, over in Mr. Froggatt's room. The third-years were looking after the

CO as he saw new patients, and helping in Minor Ops when they were needed.

Casualty and Outpatients were theoretically separate establishments, but they both used the same waiting hall, and we all belonged to Sister Lamont and our duties often overlapped. The only seniors who stayed with their specific jobs were Jessie Blake and Patrick M'Ghie, both senior SENs, who ran Minor Ops between them and watched over the second-year in the recovery ward. The four second-years ran round helping where they could, rallying at bottle-necks, answering silly questions in the hall and escorting admissions to the wards. Sister or one of the staff nurses was always available in the hall to direct the traffic and to keep an eye open for people who might need immediate attention.

Shut away in the steriliser steam and antiseptic smells behind the door marked *Dressings* we had very little idea what went on outside. Now and again there was a gap in the flow, a moment when we said: 'Who's next?' and nobody answered, which meant putting one's head out and rousing them up on the front row of chairs. Otherwise we were cut off from the *brouhaha* until well into lunchtime, and there was plenty of opportunity for private cogitation between the discharging ears, the stitches for removal, the children with washers on their swelling fingers or potties rammed over their heads, and the 'me plaster's too tight' brigade.

The Casualty house surgeon helped us when she wasn't tied up in Minor Ops or deputising for the CO. Janey Watts came to check on my little mastoid boy, and then stood by the rubber-topped table to steady him while I fed fresh ribbon gauze packing into his ear. 'Your mastoid bandages stay on,' she said enviously. 'Mine always come coiling off, so you do it. Nobody ever teaches us to do them properly, I can't think why.'

I said: 'Who doesn't? *I've* tried hard enough. Anyhow, Torfy's are better than mine.'

She slid a look at Torfy, over at the big steriliser. 'D'you know, I've been meaning ever since I came here to ask you what Torfy's short for. Or is it a private funny?'

13

'Oh, short for Torfrida. She loathes it.'

Janey grinned. 'Ah, Hereward the Wake's missus?'

'That's it. Her father's named Hereward and he thought it was apt. She says either he isn't much of a historian, or he only read the romantic bits.'

'Indeed,' she said. 'She was a right old whatsit, wasn't she? She dabbled in black magic, with all the trimmings, after he did the dirty on her. They reckoned she really *could* turn people into toads.'

My little boy, listening silently with his head obediently rigid, rolled up his eyes towards me. 'Was she a witch, Nurse?'

'I don't really know, Brian. Sort of.'

He sighed heavily. 'I wish *I* knew a witch.'

'Why?' I tucked in the end of his bandage and pinned it neatly over his good ear.

'I know somebody I'd like turned into a toad,' he said darkly as he scrambled down from the table. 'David Smart. Urgh! He's *horrible*. He's the horriblest boy in my school.'

That, of course, put David Leckie back into my head, and he stayed there while I scrubbed and boiled up a fresh supply of bowls and forceps, probes and receivers.

It wasn't as though it was the first time that kind of situation had cropped up. That was what troubled me. I had met him at the Rag ball, and whoever introduced us said: 'Mind your Ps and Qs, David. She's Prof. Kennedy's little girl.'

He said: '*Really?*' and swung me straight out on to the dance floor. 'I didn't know he had any.'

'Just the one,' I said. 'But don't let it inhibit you. Are you one of his students?' He was the ash-blond type who often look twenty until they are thirty. 'Or are you qualified?'

'Was. Just qualified.' He steered me into what felt like a very showy reverse turn at the corner by the band. 'And you can actually dance instead of writhing. How very pleasant!'

'What the well-bred young woman should know,' I admitted. 'My mother was a great believer in sending me to all the proper classes.' That made me think, momentarily, of Ted

14

Gaunt, and I went on talking to blot him out. 'Not that they made any real difference. There's not much opportunity for elocution, or playing the Moonlight Sonata, or doing the double lock-step in the waltz, when you're tearing round the wards all day.'

'You're a nurse? Not at QE, surely—I've never seen you there, have I? No, I'd have remembered.'

'I'm at Fin's,' I explained. 'Father thought I'd learn more at a hospital that wasn't student-ridden, so that cut out QE and the General.'

'*Did* he?' He held me a lot closer to him. I could recognise the tang of Old Spice now, and I felt his hand pressing warmly into the small of my back. 'Then your education must have been a little one-sided. All work and no play, and so forth. Are you SRN? No, you're not old enough.'

'Not yet. I take my finals next year.'

He led me off the floor when the music stopped. 'Let's go and find a drink ... And what next? After you qualify, I mean.'

Until then I hadn't thought about that very deeply. I had always been too busy. Too happy, too, to look far ahead. 'Go on nursing,' I said. 'Maybe I'll join the QAs or something. But I'll do some staffing at Fin's first.'

'You should come to QE. I've just landed myself a house spot—in your father's firm.' He managed to reach over several heads, and passed me a tall, cold glass. 'Vodka and lemonade?'

'Oh, but I don't——' I looked at it again, decided it was well diluted, and sampled it. It tasted of nothing in particular. 'I don't really drink,' I explained.

'Pretty weak,' David said. 'You won't get tight on *that*.'

That was what he thought. By the time I had finished the glassful I had begun to feel pretty odd. I know now that it must have been a strong mixture, but I was too inexperienced to know the difference. 'It's terribly hot in here, isn't it?' I gave him the empty glass. 'Could we go out and get some air?'

That too was the voice of inexperience. David obviously saw it as some kind of invitation. Three minutes later I was

15

fighting him off in the back of his father's sober blue Rover 2000. I understood then why he had borrowed it, why he had said: 'The Sprite wouldn't be adequate on Rag night,' when he unlocked it. 'I'm not going to *hurt* you,' he kept saying. 'Relax, sweetie! Why the panic?'

I pushed his hands away again. 'I'm *not* panicking. I just don't want this dress crushed, that's all ... And I don't want to be kissed, either.'

'You're just playing hard to get, aren't you?' He began to stroke my bare shoulder with one fingertip. 'You're out of date, my poppet. That technique went out years ago ... Ah, was it an old-fashioned little thing, then?'

'Let's go back,' I said. I was still trying to be polite. I wrenched the door open and scrambled out. The cold air hit me as if I had walked into a plate glass window, and I leaned giddily on the Rover's bonnet. David came to put his arms round me again.

This time he was gentler. 'Ups-a-daisy,' he said. 'Just hang on to me, sweetie. Take it easy.' And then he put one hand under my chin and kissed me. I struggled at first, and then—because somehow my legs didn't seem to relate to me any more, and because if I opened my eyes the headlights on the road below made gyrating Catherine wheels in my head—I stopped fighting and let him go on kissing me. Part of me even began to enjoy it, while another stood back and watched. This time it was he who broke away for breath. 'So you *are* a tease, after all,' he said softly. 'Clare, when can I see you again? Hm?' He ran one hand stealthily over my hip, slid it towards my knee, and wound his fingers tightly into the thin ninon folds of my skirt.

He was no longer David Leckie. He was Ted Gaunt. He was fourteen years old, and I was twelve, and I was terrified. The glass bubble was shattered instantly. I kicked out at him involuntarily, the way I'd kicked out at Ted Gaunt. Then I ran stumbling back to the dance floor, where there were people, lights, voices, safety.

Torfy, dancing with Sam Eales—he was Mr. Lyle-Johnson's houseman then—saw me and broke away from him.

16

'What's wrong?' she asked. 'You look as if you'd been chased by a mad bull! Calm down, mate. Here, sit down ... Now, what *is* it?'

'That—that hateful boy,' I said. 'David something.'

'David Leckie? But he's dishy!'

'He's a—an *animal*,' I told her. I suppose it sounded a bit hysterical, but I meant it fervently.

Torfy sat down beside me and waved Sam away. 'Do I take it he made a pass at you? Is that what all this drama is about? Dear girl, what did you expect? If you *will* go outside with the young gentlemen at a Rag ball ...'

'I only wanted a blow of air.'

She let out a long breath. 'That's what they all say, ducky ... Never mind, I take it that you virtuously repulsed him, and that there's no real harm done.'

'Of course I did! What do you take me for?'

'What *he* took you for is more to the point.' Torfy went on looking at me in a way that for her was positively motherly. 'There's no "of course" about it. There are those among us who wouldn't have, virtuously or otherwise, and well you know it.'

My face was hot with shame and indignation. 'Oh, people like Betsy Turnall!' Betsy was the focus of most of the grapevine scandal at that time, just after her face-saving marriage to a fifth-year from QE. 'Don't put the rest of us in *her* category.'

'No.' Torfy was perfectly serious. '*Not* people like Betsy Turnall. Ordinary people. Like you and me, for example. Just people who enjoy petting in cars, that's all. And a lot of perfectly ordinary and quite nice people do, you know. In fact they always did.'

'But you don't.' I couldn't imagine what she was trying to prove. '*You* don't, Torfy.'

'Don't I? How can you be sure? I've had my moments—though I admit I've always been pretty selective. And I've always had well-defined limits ... You know, I don't suppose the poor lad meant to eat you alive. He isn't a fish. We all need a little warmth at times. I dare say he's quite a nice chap, as chaps go. After all, he's one of your father's young gents. Is he

17

likely to take liberties if he thinks they'll be unwelcome? ...
You did *ask* for it, Clare. That's the trouble with men: you
have to watch what you ask for, because they're only too ready
to be little gentlemen and supply it.'

'Not all of them,' I said.

'*All* of them, without exception ... I sometimes think that
the nicer they are the readier they are to oblige.'

She didn't sound as if she was in contact with reality at all,
as I knew it. 'Do you know, Torfy, I don't think you and I can
possibly meet the same people every day. Our house chaps
wouldn't behave like that.'

This time she frankly laughed out loud. 'No? What about
the CO?'

I thought of Kenyon Fiske. He was small and slight, with
too much lank dark hair and one of those Asiatic drooping
moustaches, and I had never liked him. 'Ken Fiske? *I've* never
had any trouble with him.'

'Yet,' she said. 'And Matt Affleck, and Jim Kane?'

'But they're registrars. They wouldn't ... Besides, Jim
Kane's married.'

Torfy went on shaking her head very slowly. At last she
said: 'You know, for a girl who's always near the top of every
test our set has, who ran away with the Medicine prize and
who managed to land a silver medal, you really do have a lot
to learn. It must be nice to be so naïve. Everything comes as
such a surprise to you, doesn't it? ... And I suppose you've
been drinking, too? That wouldn't help.'

'It was mostly lemonade,' I said defensively. 'I couldn't
taste anything else.'

'Was it? If it was like the one I saw him fetch it was about
sixty per cent raw vodka ... Which you *can't* taste, or did you
know that?'

I wanted to cry, to hide. 'I don't know anything. I wish I'd
never come to the stupid dance. Let's go back to Fin's.'

'What? After we crawled to Matron for late leave till one
o'clock? You're joking, of course ... No, but you're not, are
you? Look, if you really want to go I'll find somebody nice to
drive you. A taxi'd be too pricey.'

'I can pay,' I said stubbornly. Six of us had come in Sam's big car, and had planned to go back that way.

Torfy was practical, as usual. 'No, you can't. You've only got fifteen bob till pay-day, remember? You stay right here. I've just remembered something a chap told me. Now don't *move*.'

She came back with a tall serious-looking young man. Well-brushed brown hair and thoughtful grey eyes, I took in that much. Not so very young, as he came closer. Thirty-odd. 'This is Neil,' she said. 'Friend of brother Mick's. The soul of reliability, and he goes our way home.'

He smiled faintly. 'I'm off almost at once, if you could use a lift. I promised to stand in for a GP by eleven-thirty, so that he can collect his wife from some bridge party and stay for drinks ... My car's right outside if you'd like to get your coat.'

It was easy with his hand under my elbow. I got the impression that he would be easy to dance with too, because he moved lightly without fuss. He drove that way too. Halfway to Fin's he said: 'I don't want to pry, Clare, but Torfy Bates said you were a bit upset. Anything I can do?'

'You've done it already,' I told him.

'Oh?'

'Just reassured me.' I think I was rapidly sobering up, if the innocent-looking drink I'd had really was the trouble. 'I got scared, that's all. It was silly of me.'

'Not silly. You're not the kind to be silly, surely?'

'But I *am*. Torfy would tell you so. She says I play Caldwell to her Sharples. She sees me as too naïve and innocent for words, I think.'

'Is innocence a fault?'

'Ignorance, then.'

He smiled at the dark windscreen. 'You mean she doesn't think you're very worldly-wise, is that it?'

I thought about that. With this man, I felt, I had to be sure what I meant. 'If being worldly-wise means being—well, mauled in the backs of cars, then I'm glad I'm not.'

'Ah, I understand now.'

'But you don't.' For some reason it seemed important to me that he should. I must still have had some of that drink circulating, or I couldn't have felt that about a stranger. He sat there very quietly, very relaxed, and it welled up from me, from my memory, without my will. 'When I was twelve, there was a boy named Ted Gaunt...We went to the same dancing class.'

'Yes,' he said. It wasn't a question, it was acceptance.

'He—he was supposed to see me home. My mother said it wasn't safe, crossing the park alone...' I had never before spoken of it to anyone, or expected to do so. Not even to Torfy, and certainly not to Mother. But I told him all about Ted, and that dreadful moment in the woods when I hadn't the remotest idea what he meant to do, and I was convinced that he intended to kill me. 'I screamed and screamed,' I said. 'And two fishermen came running up from the lake, and he ran away ... You know, I was sure they'd saved my life.'

'Poor child ... I can well imagine how you felt.'

I think he could. He was that kind of man. It seemed to me that he would be a good doctor, too. And he didn't laugh. Even when I said: 'This will sound idiotic, but I think maybe I've been a bit affected by it ever since. Because tonight when—when I was scared it all came into my mind again ... Torfy must think I'm cracked.'

'She doesn't. She's just concerned ... She warned me, by the way, not to try to kiss you goodnight.' He sounded amused. 'I promise I won't.'

I drew back to look at him. All I could see was a dark profile. 'But you wouldn't have done, anyhow, would you?'

'I might. If I thought you were the kind of girl who'd expect it. Has it ever occurred to you that we spend a lot of time trying to work out what girls *do* expect of us?'

That puzzled me. 'Then how can you tell?'

'Oh...' He smiled, watching the road. 'You can tell.'

'Then is Torfy the sort who'd expect it?'

'Heavens, no! I should imagine one'd get one's face slapped.'

'But she said——'

20

'What people say doesn't necessarily mean very much. You have to watch what they do.'

I wondered whether that applied to what *he* had said, and I kept quiet for a few minutes. After a while I said: 'I suppose I really need a course in psychology or something. You must think me pretty dim.'

'Must I?' He pulled up at the OP gate. 'Will this do you, Clare? I really ought to press on, or I'll be late.'

'Thank you *very* much,' I said. 'I'm sorry if I was a bore.' When he leaned across me to open the door I noticed that his hair grew to a point at the back of his neck. According to Torfy that meant something, but I couldn't remember what. 'Goodnight, Neil.'

'You weren't,' he said. 'Goodnight, Clare.'

I never saw him again, and I didn't ask Torfy about him either. In any case she came back so full of 'Sam says' and 'Matt thinks' that I didn't need to do any of the talking for days, and by then I realised that I'd made a fool of myself.

I had time to remember all that while I was clearing up in the dressings section, waiting for the others to come back from lunch, so that Johnny Winter and I could go. I had all the instruments cleaned and boiled, and the tables scrubbed down, by the time they came, and was straightening my cap ready to go. The new disposable caps looked smart enough at a distance, but they felt cheap and nasty, and there was no longer the special satisfaction of ironing the old lawn ones ourselves, and making them up in our own almost imperceptibly different ways.

Torfy came up behind me and talked into the mirror. 'Off you go. By the way, there's a party on Saturday, in the residents' common-room. Ken Fiske's farewell.'

On the way up to the dining-room I repeated that to Johnny. 'Ah yes,' he said. 'He finishes this week. I'd forgotten. Well, long time no party—I suppose we may as well go. You'll go, won't you?'

I wasn't wildly enthusiastic. Residents' parties can be fairly rowdy, and there was always the danger that one might get caught in their quarters. The common-room was strictly out of bounds for us. Miss Tetlow had tended to turn a blind eye, but the Deputy was less accommodating. And none of us yet knew where Miss Macintosh stood. 'I've not yet been invited,' I temporised.

'But you will be. All the Cas people will be expected to turn up.'

'Depends on the new timetable,' I reminded him. 'One of us will be on nights, for a start.'

'Don't you *want* to go?'

'Not specially, no,' I said.

I didn't know it, but I was to regret that remark before the week was out.

CHAPTER 2

AFTER lunch I tracked Torfy down as she toured the department, collecting bits and pieces for her OP session. I had already done my own foraging, making sure of an ophthalmoscope and a sphyg for mine. The trouble is that every consultant has his own fads; and that he doesn't understand that pieces of equipment get redistributed during the week, and don't sit idly in his room awaiting his return. Torfy was already grasping a patella hammer and a tape-measure and was frowning into one of the cupboards looking for something else.

'Now that you've been mathematical about it,' I said, 'how does it stand?'

'The timetable?' She sounded abstracted. 'Oh, we've got it worked out. But only in terms of Nurses A, B, C and so on. Sister hasn't put names to them yet. Why?'

'I was wondering who'll be first to nights?'

'Thinking about the party?'

I said yes, that was the general idea.

'Then tell Sister. Maybe she'll put Luke on. He's not much of a party-goer. Anyhow, he grouses whatever happens—that boy is a natural depressive, if you ask me—so he may as well have something to grouse *about*. Ask her. She can only say "no".'

That wasn't quite the object of the exercise. 'But neither am I. Much of a party-goer, I mean. Actually I was thinking of volunteering.'

She turned round from the instrument cabinet to look me over. She had on her despairing expression, which involved shaking her head at every inch of me, from feet progressing slowly to cap, finishing with a jerk of the chin and a quick upwards roll of the eyes. 'Clare, you know what? You're getting more and *more* anti-social. You'll end up another Tetlow, shut up in an office, if you're not damn careful.'

'I wouldn't mind that,' I said. 'It would be very peaceful. I could have cosy games of chess with the SMO, and keep my ear to the ground in the nicest possible way.'

'Well, get it to the ground now, dear girl, and find out who the new CO will be. Nobody knows. It *was* to have been this Alan Worcester the chaps were talking about, but he's gone down with typhoid in Bahrein, or somewhere equally inconvenient, and they've had to whip up the short-list again. So the SSO told Jeremy.'

'There you are, you see. You know far more than I do about it. As usual.'

'If you'd do a little more mingling, love, you'd hear more ... Whose OP are you taking?'

'Dr. Monahan,' I said. 'Why?'

'I've got the orthopods. Mr. Pettifer's all very well, but that new registrar of his terrifies me. She's so *big*. You get the feeling that she wouldn't hesitate to chuck you straight out at the window if you did the wrong thing. She could, too.'

I thought of Leonora Kirk, every inch of five-eleven, with muscles and a personality to match. 'You need to be, if you're an orthopaedist. She's all right. She just over-compensates. Inside, or that's my theory, there's a little Twiggy type trying to get out. You just take her as she comes.'

'Then let's swop?'

She was teasing. 'What? Miss my lovely Dr. Monahan? Not likely.'

'He's an old dodderer.'

'He is not! He's very sweet.'

Torfy's smile was sardonic. 'And he does have Toby Jarrett as a registrar? Go on, we know what the attraction is.'

That interested me very much, because I had been trying for a week or two to discover—without asking, which would be cheating—who had replaced Jeremy Gibbon in her design for living, as Jeremy had replaced a temporary Australian anaesthetist, who had replaced Sam Eales. Torfy, interested in a fresh male, became enigmatic. Unlike Sally Dane she never took a brass band with her when she went hunting. It seemed to me that it was high time to put her in the picture where Toby was concerned; I'd meant to before, but somehow it had slipped my mind. 'I'm not in the least interested in Toby,' I established first. Then I broke the news. 'In any case, he's committed, isn't he?'

She frowned at Mr. Pettifer's tape-measure round her hips, and then ran it carefully back into its metal case. 'Since when? I can't really have put on two inches, can I?'

'He was telling Dr. Monahan last week that he's getting engaged to Leila Hamilton. I meant to tell you.' There was no point in not being explicit.

She brought out the tape again and bent to run it round one ankle. 'Well, that's no bigger, at any rate ... He is? Isn't that typical?' She straightened up, pink in the face. 'You do mean Dr. Hamilton's daughter? Talk about a *mariage de convenance*! How glad I am that I'm not an arch-quack's child! Nobody could say that a village schoolmaster for a pa was bait. Girls with consultant daddies must spend their time suspecting their lovers' motives.'

That was well below the belt. 'Thanks!' I said. 'So reassuring.'

Torfy lifted both hands six inches or so and dropped them to her sides again. 'Oh, I'm *sorry*! Wasn't thinking. You know I didn't mean *you*, you dimwit.'

'No. But it applies, doesn't it?'

'Dear girl, the chap who marries you will do it for your sterling worth, as Miss Tetlow would say. It's only the dumbies who land ambitious husbands by virtue of being Daddy's daughter.'

She really was floundering now. 'Leila Hamilton's no dumbie. She's a Ph.D. among other things.'

'Yes, dear. And she looks it. That's what I mean—Toby isn't after her for her sex-appeal, and he isn't the kind to go for a blue-stocking. So what else is there? Daddy.' There was no doubt about it, Torfy was hurt and undermined. It wasn't like her to indulge in woolly thinking. Or to leap to conclusions before she'd personally ferreted out every last fact.

'You don't know,' I told her. 'He's not daft himself, and he likes girls who know what he's talking about.' There was no need to spell it out, but I did. 'Girls like you, for example. And maybe he was hyperbolising after all. Maybe she won't have him. Anyhow, she hasn't got him to the altar yet, and no engagement's been actually announced, so as far as you know he's still footloose, isn't he?'

'God,' she said, looking out into the hall. 'Here comes that Amazonian woman, and I've not even set her table yet. I'm off. See you.'

'Me too,' I said.

I knew Dr. Monahan's room was ready: I'd already checked that. My next job was to get the names of the waiting patients—there were already a dozen sitting outside his door—and find their treatment folders to accompany them. The folders were all in a big filing drawer lifted to a table immediately outside his door. Horace, our nicest little porter, had put the drawer out for me, and later he would carry it back to its place in the bank of cabinets along the end of the hall.

He had already found the first six folders for me. He pushed them into my hand. 'Here's the first few, Nurse. They're in the right order. I've got Mr. Andrews and Mr. Fox into the cubicles for you to get themselves ready.'

Horace was a treasure. Torfy had William, twice as big and only half as helpful. I was lucky. 'Bless you,' I said. 'Dr. Monahan hasn't come, has he?'

'Not yet, Nurse. I'd have fetched you. Dr. Jarrett isn't in, either. Meeting the Chief in the car park, I dare say.'

I put the first two folders on Dr. Monahan's desk in the inner room. They were both new patients and he would want to see them himself. The next four were old patients, and their cards didn't have the stamped purple star that merited the attention of the great man in person. They would be seen by Toby Jarrett, in the outer room.

I settled Mr. Andrews in the consulting-room when he had stripped off and put on an examination robe, and brought in the next new one to his cubicle as a replacement. While I waited I checked on the supply of clean sheets for the couches. These too, I saw, were now of the disposable type. I remarked on it to Horace outside, and he said: 'Yes, I brought a stack of them across from stores. Well, as long as they don't go inventing disposable nurses...'

'I wouldn't put it past them to programme robots one day,' I said. 'Or train chimpanzees. With recruiting at an all-time low they'll have to do *something*.'

'How about the "tender loving care", then, Nurse? No, I don't reckon chimps'd have the touch. Here's another six folders for you ... No, don't thank me. I'm just keeping out of the CO's way, to tell the truth. Not in a very happy mood, we aren't, this afternoon.'

'Oh? How's that?' I smiled at the front-row patients to show them I had them well in mind. Two of them smiled back; the rest went on studying my shoes in that disconcerting way they have. 'Well, Sister's not a lady to wrap things up, is she, Nurse? And he *was* very late coming down. All behind with his new ones, he is.'

I could imagine what Sister Lamont, who was always pro-patient, had said to Kenyon Fiske. She had never been one of his admirers—if indeed he had any—and she wouldn't be sorry to see him go. She felt that he left far too much of his work to Janey Watts, for one thing. 'That gairr-l's soft!' she told me once. Her accent was always noticeable when she was moved. 'She puts in eighteen hours a day, and never grumbles. She desairr-ves a better deal.' Then the final scathing comment, rare from her. 'That man is a *rr-at*, Nurse.'

'Ah, well,' I told Horace. 'He'll be off on Saturday. You don't happen to know——'

'No, I don't, Nurse ... Here's Doctor, now, and Dr. Jarrett with him.'

They looked like a couple of Vikings coming across the hall together. Torfy has a theory that the Vikings were narrow and dark, and drags in the Highland Scots to prove it, but I have always imagined them tall, fair, bearded and blue-eyed, with a Player's sailor look about them. I held open the door for Dr. Monahan, who smiled politely through his blond-grey beard, and let Toby, grinning through his curly gold one, hold it for me. I followed the Chief to the inner room and left Toby momentarily to sort himself out. 'This is Mr. Andrews,' I said as I took his jacket and tied his OP gown. 'Query Addison's, sent in by Dr. Fussell of Chester Road. His specimen shows a trace of albumen, that's all. And there's a letter on your blotter, sir.'

He nodded benignly. 'Thank you so much, Nurse. Now, Mr. Andrews, will you just lie on the couch for me, please?'

I settled Mr. Andrews with his modesty blanket, and went back to Toby to get the flow going. All afternoon I shuttled patients in and out, tested specimens, directed people to X-ray, the path. lab or the dispensary, and settled arguments about priorities among the waiters outside. Neither the appointments system—which they completely ignored—nor the star-coding—which the non-stars bitterly resented—meant as much to them as the jungle principle of first-come-first-served. Every quarter of an hour or so there was a wail of: 'I was here long before that feller!' so that I had to explain that that feller was either a new patient or a star, or that the complainant was here an hour ahead of his appointment. The trouble was that they all wanted to see Dr. Monahan personally, and it couldn't be done.

'You get better fast,' I told them. 'And then you'll see Him Himself to be discharged. Or develop a new unheard-of disease, and then he'll see you.'

We got through them all eventually, in spite of the fresh supplies who kept coming along from the registration office, and by half past five even Dr. Monahan was ready to go. OPs were supposed to finish at five, but they never did. The slower ones, like Mr. Lyle-Johnson, often went on until six, and there was a legend that a locum registrar left to cope during Mr. Huxley's holidays, when only non-stars attended, had actually spun it out until seven-fifteen.

Toby hung back a moment to say: 'Party Sunday. Fiske's ta-ta do. OK?'

'I know,' I said. 'But are we all invited?'

'Well, you are. You and Torfy Bates, I mean. He asked me to say so.'

Somehow he didn't sound like a man about to affiance himself to Leila Hamilton or anyone else. Surely a hospital bunfight wouldn't take precedence over weekending with the top brass, I thought; and Dr. Hamilton's weekend hospitality was a thing one didn't turn down, in any case, because it was known to be pretty well a royal command. Sister Woolley had once declined, pleading a previous engagement, and had never been invited again. His other ward sister, Gippy Hayward, had set aside a family wedding to go, and continued to be included every six weeks or so. Yet here was Toby making sure that Torfy went to Ken Fiske's party: I knew he wasn't in the least interested in me. I said: 'Thanks, Toby. I'll tell Torfy you said so.'

He smiled. 'Yes, do that small thing.'

When I had cleared up the rooms, re-filed the folders, and sent Horace off with request forms to all the right places, I went across to Sister's office. I'd been on duty since half past seven, it was nearly six, and I was beginning to flag. It seemed far more than a week since my last days off. I found the new timetable pinned behind the door and noted that Sally Dane was down for the first stint of nights. Sister had gone, and Jessie Blake was sitting at her table filling in date cards for

28

Colonel Findlay-Smith's dental sessions. She looked up at me after a moment or two. 'It's all right, Kennedy. You'll be able to go to the party. If you like that kind of thing.'

The thought again failed to excite me. 'Yes,' I said. 'Any drums for sterilising, Jessie? I'll drop them in the autoclave room as I go.'

'There's a trolleyful, love. Would you mind? If they go now the theatre people'll shove them through with theirs. I hear we shan't have this game much longer: Miss Macintosh is campaigning for a central sterile supply department.' She glanced up at the wall clock. 'Five to. You may as well clear off if you're ready. I'll be another quarter of an hour yet. Who's staying late tonight—Bates?'

Only one of us was ever on the ten-thirty to nine shift, to hold the fort until the night people came on. I checked with the current timetable. 'Luke Martin,' I said. 'Why?'

'I'd better stay on with him for a bit, I think. The police have rung—there's a coach crash on A5 and they may have to shed some of the casualties this way.'

I turned back. 'Look, I'll stay! I'm not doing anything. And you're not supposed to be a Casualty wallah.'

'Oh, buzz off!' she said. 'You came on an hour earlier than I did. What are you trying to prove? That you're an SRN?'

That did it. Jessie might be an SEN, but she was a better nurse than plenty of SRNs I'd known. If all our SENs had been like her we should have clamoured for more of them. The trouble was that a lot of the SENs who worked in the wards were still the qualified-by-experience kind. They were getting on in years, and while some of them were wonderful practical nurses there were still a few whose alleged experience had taught them less than nothing, and who were incapable of learning. Or maybe they felt it was all too late. But the only reason Jessie wasn't SRN and SCM was that she had come into nursing after an early marriage, and couldn't desert her husband and baby for a full three-year training. 'Don't you dare be like that,' I told her. 'All right, I know when I'm not wanted.' We grinned at one another to show that there were no hard feelings.

29

I collected the drum trolley from outside the theatre and trundled it up the ramp towards the autoclave room. Ken Fiske overtook me just before the steep bit and said: 'Let me help you, my flower.' But his idea of helping was to push with one arm round my waist, until I moved aside. 'You'll be coming to my thrash on Saturday, won't you?'

I looked at him distastefully. His yellow-brown eyes were exactly level with mine, and his hair needed a trim. 'Maybe,' I said. 'Depends how things work out. We've a new timetable to implement, you know. Night duty for the masses, and so on.'

'Now don't be that way!' He took his hand away from the trolley and patted me on my *gluteus maximus* muscles. I stiffened from head to foot, but he didn't notice that. 'You know I want you to come.' He repeated the pat, only this time his hand lingered.

I stopped walking at once. 'Don't *do* that!'

'What? Oh, *that*.' He did it again.

He was directly behind the trolley, on the steep part of the slope. I simply had to let it go, stand aside and let it run on to his feet. I hoped it hurt. 'Now will you keep your hands to yourself?' I was blazing with annoyance, and I felt slightly sick. His touch had that effect.

He laughed. He was the thick-skinned kind that had to come back for more. '*What* are you? Say three times after me: "I am a little spitfire." Naughty temper!' He disentangled his feet and began to push the trolley again. 'Why the touch-me-not stuff?'

I breathed deeply. 'I'm supposed to be a nurse. You're supposed to be a doctor. Perhaps you could manage a little method acting and play it that way? Scene, a hospital corridor, in case you'd forgotten.'

After that he sulked, and let me push the trolley by myself. 'Quite,' he told my back. 'And that thing on your head is supposed to be a cap, a paper one at that, not a ruddy halo. What a little prig you really are, Clare. I don't know why any of us bother.'

'I'm sorry,' I said. 'But you know perfectly well that I detest being touched. It's not as though I hadn't told you before. But it doesn't seem to register, does it? I can't help it. That's the way I am.'

'Then maybe you should talk to Rothwell Green,' he told me, as he turned off for the residents' corridor. There was a nasty little edge on his voice when he said that. Obviously it was meant as a snide remark, but it conveyed less than nothing to me.

I pushed the drums into the autoclave room. Staff Price was in there, unloading the stuff for the top theatres. Through the steam and clangour I asked her: 'Who or what is Rothwell Green? It ought to ring a bell, but it doesn't?'

'Rothwell Green?' She frowned, and took off her heavy gauntlets. 'Shove that lot in, if you like. Watch your hands— it's hellish hot ... Oh, he's a psychiatrist at QE, isn't he? He comes here now and again if he's called in.' She looked at my face. 'Why do you ask?'

'Nothing. Doesn't matter.' I began loading Jessie Blake's drums into the monster. I caught my wrist a couple of times before I had the sense to put the gloves on. I suppose I must have been throwing the stuff in pretty savagely, because after a while Price said: 'Hey! Penny for them, Kennedy. Just who are you mentally thumping?'

'My pet abomination,' I said unhelpfully, and went on slinging.

I caught Torfy up on the Home stairs. 'Message for you,' I told her. 'Yet another about this party tomorrow.'

'How many more?' she said. 'They certainly don't slack when it comes to spreading the news, do they? I've already been told by Ken Fiske, Janey Watts, Jeremy Gibbon, the SSO and at least a dozen nurses.'

'Oh well, this makes a change. Toby Jarrett this time.'

Torfy has a curtain she pulls, the way birds of prey veil their eyes. 'Oh, him. Where did you get to at six o'clock? Jessie said you'd gone on.'

'Autoclave room, and having a difference of opinion with the CO,' I explained. 'Toby said that you and I were specially

31

invited. But he meant you.'

Her face was pink, and that was most unusual. 'Oh, rot! What was all that about the CO?'

'He asked me to be sure to tell you.'

'Who, Fiske?'

'No, Toby.'

'So you've told me. Now tell me about this little tiff you had with Fiske.'

We came to a halt outside her bedroom door. 'Oh, nothing. He says I'm a prig.'

'Oh, *does* he? Well, we can't all have the Sally Dane technique, can we?'

'Would we want to?'

'Would we *need* to, is more the point ... Listen, Clare——' She unlocked her door. 'Come in for a minute. My feet are killing me—I can't talk standing up.'

I sat on her bed and waited. 'Well? You were saying?'

'Ah yes.' She took off her cap, unclipped her belt and began to brush her hair. In the half-light it glimmered like black-shot-green cockerel's feathers. 'This Leila Hamilton thing.'

I had been wondering how long she would manage to hold out. 'What about it?'

She went on peering into the mirror. 'What exactly did Toby *say*? Last Thursday, was it?'

I calculated. 'Yes. Oh, it was after we'd finished. I was out in the hall, filing folders, and they were jawing over their tea. When I went back again Dr. Monahan was just saying: "Really? And who is the fortunate young woman, my boy?" So Toby said it was Leila Hamilton, and——'

'For Pete's sake! Can't you give it in direct speech?'

'Let me think ... Toby said: "Dr. Hamilton's daughter, sir. Leila." So Dr. Monahan said: "Leila Hamilton, eh? Splendid, splendid! A *very* suitable match." Well, then they saw me and clammed up. That's all.'

'Yes, but before Dr. Monahan asked who the girl was.'

'I've no idea. I wasn't there, was I? But Toby was sort of beaming with pleasure, so what else was I to think? ... On the other hand...' I was remembering Toby's expression when he

32

had said: 'Do that small thing.'

'What?' Torfy turned round at last. 'On the other hand?'

'Well . . . I think you should go to the party.'

'I mean to. *And* you're going, if I have to drag you there by the hair, my girl.'

'We'll see,' I said. 'Can I borrow your bath oil? Mine's leaked into my sponge bag, what there was of it. I'm going to have an early night. How about you?'

Torfy never stayed in if she could help it. She said she needed to go out and look at people who weren't nurses or doctors, and when she had no date—which wasn't very often—she liked to prowl round the coffee bars and talk to strangers. When she had free mornings she went to magistrates' courts. It was interesting, she said, and warmer than the reference library for resting the feet in. But this time she surprised me by saying: 'Me too. I'm whacked.' Torfy was never whacked; her energy was phenomenal and, coupled with her skinniness, made me wonder sometimes whether she was slightly hyperthyroid.

On Friday afternoon I took the gynae clinic. Little Mr. Lyle-Johnson was a kindly and conscientious man who saw almost every patient himself. Only those whom he considered malingerers—most of them complained of low backache, which is next to impossible to disprove—were denied stars on their cards. This meant that in spite of a complicated appointments system there was inevitably a build-up of custom on the rows of chairs outside his door, and some of the patients became extremely fractious. Women are more vocal than men, even without a grievance; with one their murmurings seemed on Fridays to increase by the square of the inexorable increase in their numbers. It is an odd fact, probably known only to nurses, that while gynae wards are notoriously the gayest in a hospital—sometimes to a Rabelaisian degree—their OPs are always the most miserable. I had a theory that in the wards they were thoroughly enjoying, even when in considerable pain and discomfort, their enforced freedom from housekeeping; whereas when they were attending OP they were at the stage of finding it all too much of a drag, whether pre-op or post-op, and that they would only cheer up when either admitted or exempted from the weekly trek.

Because I sympathised with two young women who had to meet children from the local infants' school I allowed them—unobtrusively, I thought—to jump the queue. It was a mistake. The mutterings became open rebellion. Every one of the other patients claimed to have incontrovertible reasons for being seen out of turn. If it wasn't 'me old man's tea' it was the scarcity of number nine buses, or there was a hire-car waiting, or the corner shop would be shut. It happened every time I took Mr. Lyle-Johnson's clinic, and every time I swore that I would never again do favours. They were as competitive as children.

Apart from the complaints in the hall this situation also meant that Jeremy Gibbon, the registrar, had practically nothing to do once he had disposed of the non-stars—to the annoyance of the privileged, who had a great deal longer to wait—and he couldn't even pass the time by talking to me, because I had to chaperone every patient who was examined. He did test some of the specimens for me, but he was far too thorough and wasted a lot of time looking for occult blood, and other exoticisms, when all I wanted was a quick check for albumen and sugar, so that I still had most of them to run in myself.

We might all have become tired and irritable, like the patients outside, but for Mr. Lyle-Johnson's unfailing good temper and perfect manners. Eventually Jeremy, bored to tears, said: 'Well, L-J's doing most of the work, so if he can take it we can. But for God's sake get the little man to knock off for some tea—it's twenty to six.'

'Yell for Horace,' I told him hurriedly as I chased the next patient through. 'He'll fetch some.'

'Not for me, he won't.'

'Say it's for me, then.'

The patient, who had been grumbling her head off out in the hall, looked at me apologetically. 'Haven't you had no tea, love? *I've* been down to the canteen twice.'

I didn't point out that doubtless that was why she had been

34

missing when I'd called her name, and why she was late getting in. I contented myself with saying that we didn't expect any on Fridays. After she had been examined, and was dressed again, I left her with L-J while I raced through to see if the next patient was ready. What she had said to him in my absence I could only imagine because he called me back into the room as I ushered her out and said: 'Nurse, I've been *very* remiss. It's extremely late, and we've been working for nearly four hours, and I don't believe you've even had a cup of tea. Do you think you could procure some, for yourself and me, and Mr. Gibbon?'

I smiled. 'The porter's bringing some, sir.'

'Splendid! You should really remind me of these lapses of mine, Nurse ... Well now, who is the next patient?'

I passed him the folder. 'Mrs. Fellowes. Post-op check, hysterectomy six weeks ago ... She's complaining of backache, sir. Actually I think she's one of the sort who get at the housework too soon. It can't be easy, with five children. Perhaps you could have a word with the husband, sir? He's out in the hall.'

'What a good idea, Nurse. Indeed I will. But why is he here? Not working?'

That was one of the things I liked about Mr. Lyle-Johnson. With all his public school ability to turn the blindest of eyes on occasion he still took cues beautifully and was invariably on the ball. 'No, sir. Not for several months.'

'You'd like me to read the riot act, I expect.'

'If you will, sir. I think she'd be grateful.'

There was a smile in his voice. 'Yes. When she's dressing you wheel him through, please. You could usefully bring my tea at that point, too. I always find myself giving it away if it comes in with a patient.'

I had sometimes wondered about that. 'Yes, sir.' I went to fetch Mrs. Fellowes. Later, when she was getting dressed, and I had taken her husband through, I told Jeremy: 'Look out for flying bodies. L-J's laying down the law.'

'To that Stan Ogden type you just took in? *Does* he?'

It hadn't happened since Jeremy had come over from

general surgery to the gynae scene, I realised. 'Oh yes. But only to husbands. And never in front of their wives. He's a gentleman.'

He rolled his eyes at me over the edge of his cup. 'Define a gentleman, young Kennedy.'

'I don't know who said it ... but "a man who is rude only on purpose". Sounds like Oscar Wilde, but it probably wasn't. It suits L-J, anyway.'

'Yes, I like that one. And a lady?'

I was too tired to think, and he obviously had some gem ready to trot out. 'You tell me.'

'I heard a good definition the other day: "A lady is a woman who makes a man want to behave like a gentleman." No? What's *that* look for?'

'So if a man doesn't behave in a gentlemanly way towards me, then it's because I'm no lady? Is that what you're saying?'

'Presumably ... Oh, you don't agree, do you?'

I thought of Ken Fiske, and David Leckie, and Ted Gaunt, and a lot of other people. Where had I gone wrong? 'No, I don't.'

'Well, give me an example.'

'All right. If a man makes a pass at me, and it's unwelcome, is it *my* fault?'

'Of course it is.' He was laughing at me. Jeremy looked about twelve when he laughed, although the rest of the time he gave the impression of being older than he was. At forty-one he was the eldest of Fin's registrars, but only because he refused to apply for a consultancy. He had his Fellowship before the SSO did, but at that point his ambition seemed to have fizzled out. 'Of course it's your fault. If you don't want the chaps to notice you, young Kennedy, you should go round in a false moustache, and one of those hideous dressing-gowns this establishment sees fit to issue to the X-ray department. What do you expect? Look, a man meets a girl, likes the look of her, wants to show her that he finds her attractive. Perfectly natural. Well, what is he supposed to do?'

'He should—he should put it into words.'

'Oh, that's a counsel of perfection! Most men—*most* men

36

—are pretty inarticulate, you know. And far more afraid than you girls realise of making asses of themselves. Verbally, any-how. And they're trained practically from birth never to put anything in writing.'

'Go on,' I said. 'You haven't convinced me yet.' In fact I was more interested in Mr. Fellowes, and in letting Jeremy's rather nice voice flow over me while I waited for him, than in collecting tips about male psychology, but I listened just the same.

'Put it this way: if a chap tries to kiss a girl, say, and he gets his face slapped, that's fine. He's found out how the land lies, and he doesn't feel a fool. A slap's part of the game. But if he *tells* her—or worse still writes to her to tell her—that he thinks she's a doll, and gets shot down in flames for it, then he *does* feel cheap. Don't ask me why, because I don't know. It's a basic fact of male nature. We'd rather be slapped than slated, any day. And real nagging's simply the end.'

'Thank you,' I said. 'In future I'll take Karate lessons and save my breath ... What d'you think's going on in there? I've still four patients waiting.'

We listened, but there was not so much as a raised voice. Evidently Mr. Lyle-Johnson was using his frail-womanhood line. It was only in recalcitrant cases that he had ever been known to resort to: 'I'm warning you, Smith!' or: 'Good God, man!'

Jeremy said: 'Shall I burst in and interrupt?' but he went on leaning on his folded arms on the desk. 'Oh, I nearly forgot. While you were nattering to L-J Nurse Dane came looking for you. It *is* Dane, isn't it? The blonde with stuff round her eyes, I mean.'

'It is,' I said. 'And what did *she* want?'

'Didn't say, ducky. Wants a word before you go off.'

'She'll have gone herself by now.'

'No, she said she'd wait, actually.'

That was right out of character. Sally Dane didn't stay in the department a moment longer than she had to. 'Then it *must* be important!' I put my head out into the hall. The last two patients, not yet in the cubicles, sprang up at once. So did

37

Mrs. Fellowes. 'Nearly ready for you,' I told them. 'Mrs. Fellowes, your husband shouldn't be more than two ticks now.' Sally Dane was standing by the registration office, leaning on the closed window-hatch. I waved her over. 'Can't stop now. See you in the Home,' I told her.

She nodded. 'Don't be long. I've got a date at seven-fifteen.'

I closed the door again. The patient in the first cubicle whispered: 'Did you say take *all* my clothes off, Nurse?'

I went in to her. 'That's it—just leave your slip on, Mrs. Grove, and put this dressing-gown on. That your specimen? That's right ... Doctor won't be long.' I must have said that thirty times that afternoon.

Mr. Fellowes emerged from the consulting-room looking hangdog, and I hoped he was feeling that way. I hoped it even more after L-J. had given me a few more details. When I had rapidly tidied the couch I said: 'Next patient, sir?'

'Yes, please, Nurse.' He looked very satisfied with himself. 'I think Mr. Fellowes understood me. It seems his wife has actually been *working*—heaven knows how, poor woman— since ten days after hysterectomy! I've told him I want to see her again in a fortnight, that she's to rest until then, and that I may have to take her in again if there's no improvement.'

'Yes, sir. Thank you very much.'

'You do know what her work *is*, do you, Nurse?'

I tried to remember. 'I'm sorry, sir. I've forgotten.'

'She's a bus conductress. Up and down all those stairs, poor soul ... Well, who comes next?'

'Mrs. Grove, sir. New patient, but there's no letter.'

'No, there won't be. Her GP telephoned me.' He looked up at me. 'He wants me to terminate her pregnancy, on account of a very nasty rheumatic heart. So does her husband. She won't agree, I'm told ... Well, Nurse?'

'Sir?'

'Are you going to help me to persuade her?'

Even for L-J that wasn't on, and I think he knew it. 'No, sir, I'm not. Apart from any other consideration, if she wants to take the risk she should be allowed to. Well, *I* think so.'

'Oh, you do, do you?'

38

'I'd want to, sir. Most women would. Adoption isn't the answer to a woman who really wants a child of her own. Certainly not once she's pregnant. She'd risk anything then.'

I think he was a little surprised. He usually got one sentence at a time from me. 'Then perhaps I'd better not try?'

I smiled. 'Oh, you can try, sir. But I don't think you'll succeed, if her mind's made up.'

I was right. Twenty minutes later, when the last patient was in, Jeremy was composing a letter to Dr. Hamilton, our best heart man, asking him to hold a watching brief. 'I've met 'em before,' he said. 'Nine times out of ten their guts get them through labour with miraculous safety. A dispensation of providence, d'you think, or is it sheer bloody-minded feminine will-power?'

'Just plain faith,' I said. 'Jeremy, we've finished when this one's dressed. So will you be a dear and post the letters yourself, when you've finished them? I must see what the Dane girl wants. I can clear up in here first thing tomorrow—it's Saturday.'

'You seriously expect me to walk all the way to the front hall, carrying all——'

'Will you, or won't you?'

'Yes,' he said. 'Of course. Trot on, young Kennedy.'

I might have guessed what Sally Dane was up to. She was waiting at the bottom of the Home stairs, dressed to kill, and enclosed in a heavy aura of Primitif. Hardly a perfume for a blonde, I'd have thought, even a bottle one like her, but it was absolutely right for her. 'Look, this night-duty lark,' she began. 'I'm down for the first week, and it's quite OK except for Saturday. I do want to go to Ken's party. Johnny Winter said you weren't all that keen, so—— Well, I wondered.'

'You want me to stand in?' Johnny would, I thought.

'Well, yes.'

'What does Sister say?'

'She said that if I got a senior to cover it would be all right. But I'd got to fix it tonight, so that whoever it was could go to bed tomorrow. Then I'd do their job.'

There was more to it than that, because she kept examining

the polish on her thumb-nail instead of meeting my eyes. 'And?'

She sighed. 'Actually, she said she didn't want to have the rota mucked about a night at a time. That I really ought to find someone who'd take the whole week ... I suppose you wouldn't want to do that?'

'I would, in fact,' I said. 'But I'm doing this for me, not for you. I don't much want to go, and this gives me a watertight excuse.'

'You don't *want* to go?' The way she looked at me I might have been turning down a premium bond jackpot. 'You're an angel, Kennedy! Thanks a lot. Then I do your jobs tomorrow. What is there, specially?'

'Dressings in the morning, casualties in the afternoon. Then I'd planned to give Sister's cupboards a good turn-out.'

'Will do. Anything else?'

'Yes, I'm afraid there is. So as not to keep you hanging about I've come off without clearing up the gynae clinic. I don't know what Sister would say—but there it is. You'd better do it first thing. I'd go back and do it tonight if I thought I wouldn't get caught.'

'Right. Then I'll be off. And thanks *very* much.'

'All part of the service,' I said. I wondered what Torfy was going to say. Not that anything she could say would make any difference now. There were some things that even she couldn't reorganise, and Sister Lamont's timetable was one of them. I was another.

CHAPTER 3

I CALLED in and told Torfy as I went along to the bathrooms. She said: 'Now why did you do that? After all I said about being anti-social! You just don't listen, do you?'

'I don't know. She wants to go to the bunfight a lot more than I do, though.'

She was exasperated, as I'd known she would be. 'Of course she does! She's pursuing Ken Fiske, and this is her last chance to make it stick, you ninny. He's supposed to go to London tomorrow, isn't he? So somebody said.'

'So?' It didn't seem to me that I was the guardian of Sally Dane's destiny. 'She's very welcome. I shan't be there to see the fun, but you can tell me about it afterwards. I shall enjoy that. And you'll enjoy embroidering it a bit and bringing out the highlights. I see the pattern better when you tell me.'

Torfy took off her glasses, polished them crossly, and put them on again. She looked like an intellectual leprechaun sitting there, knees-up, on her bed. 'You're getting worse,' she told me. 'First you're anti-social, now you want to live at second hand through me. You want me to *tell* you about life, instead of experiencing it yourself. You want to withdraw from reality. There's a name for that sort of thing, you know.'

'You too?' I said. 'Ken Fiske told me I ought to see a psychiatrist. Don't you start!'

'Did he? Why?'

I told her. Then I added: 'Jeremy Gibbon says that if men take liberties it's because I'm no lady. Or words to that effect. If I carried on like Sally Dane I could understand it, but I don't.'

'No, of course you don't. But you must do *something* to them. I mean, I don't have all this trouble controlling the beasts. If Ken Fiske laid a finger on me I'd slap him hard, and he evidently knows it.'

41

'Yes. Jeremy says slapping's better than slating.'

'Oh, you've discussed it with him? You don't think, do you, that you're inclined to take it all a weeny bit too seriously, love?'

'Maybe I do,' I said. 'I don't know. How seriously do other people take it? It's something I can't help, that's all.'

Torfy had on her Clare-analysing face. I think I worried her a lot. 'You do *like* men? I mean, you enjoy their company?'

'Of course I do! I'm not odd. But I just don't want them to take it for granted that if I'm nice to them it means I want them to paw me. No doubt one day I'll meet one I'll feel differently about, and then I'll be throwing myself at him *à la* Dane. It's as simple as that.'

'Haven't you ever wanted a man to make love to you? Not even ever so slightly? ... Well, have you ever met one you wouldn't actively *shrink* from?'

I gathered my bath towel into concertina pleats and let it go again. 'Oh, there are lots I don't shrink from—but I might if they stopped being brotherly. I don't know. I've only once— well, no, not even then.'

She went on pursuing the point relentlessly. 'You've once felt you might enjoy it if he did?'

'Well, yes.'

'And?'

'What do you mean, "and"?, Torfy?'

'I mean what happened?'

'Nothing. Nothing at all.'

She frowned at me. I was being very unsatisfactory. 'But you wanted it to?'

'No, not really ... It was just that if anything *had* happened I mightn't have minded very much. I might have enjoyed it. That's as far as I can go, honestly. I must be hard to please, I suppose.'

She sighed noisily. There was no handling me, her face said. But she tried to be fair. 'No. No, you're not. You're just un-awakened. And fastidious with it. Oh well, why not? If you've met just one man you felt comfortable with, then that's all I wanted to know. I was beginning to think you were going to be anti-men for life. But maybe there's hope for you ... Do you ever see him?'

'Good lord, no.'

'Well, there must be others around somewhere just like him. All we have to do is to find them ... What sort was he—to look at?'

I humoured her, because I had no intention of telling her who it was. She would have laughed at the slightness of the contact. 'Tallish, thick brown hair. Strong-looking. Very quiet, really nice hands, I remember. Grey eyes. That's all.'

'Come on. Voice?'

'Fairly deep, but quiet. Slow. Not one of those flustery voices.'

She nodded several times. 'Sounds good and relaxed.'

'Yes,' I said. 'Yes, I think that's the word. Relaxed.'

'Precisely what you need, of course. A dedicated bird-watcher, content to sit mouse-quiet in a hide all day so as not to startle you. Patient as hell ... You don't ask much!'

I went to the door. 'I'm not the one who's doing the asking. All I want is to be left alone.'

'And I've told you, beware what you ask for from men, because they'll supply it. Ask them once too often to leave you alone and they darned well *will*. Then where will you be? Sitting in some admin office, wondering what girls are coming to these days ... Oh, I nearly forgot to tell you. What *do* you think Miss Macintosh said to the SSO?'

'Tell me. I'm too tired for games.' I leaned on the door post. 'What *did* she say?'

'That we ought to have communal parties sometimes. And she asked him whether the residents ever threw them, and he said yes, but it was all a bit illicit. So she laughed like a drain and said it was like that when she was training, but this was 1970 and times had changed, and it was quite OK by her if we went to the common-room or the men came to the rec. As long as we were all in our own quarters by midnight, and cleaned the joint up after us. But really, it's taken all the fun out of it, hasn't it?'

43

'Of course,' I said. 'And she's cute enough to know it. Very clever of her ... I'm going for a bath now, before I go to sleep standing up, like a horse.'

'*Do* they?'

'I thought you were a village girl! Will you put my name down for late breakfast?'

'In bed?'

'If you can persuade somebody to bring it, yes.'

'Sure. I'll come myself, if I can't.'

I looked forward to that. It was the only little luxury Miss Tetlow had allowed us. Even as juniors we had been able to order breakfast in bed, provided a willing friend could be pressed into service during her nine or nine-thirty lunch break. The point being that we weren't to make work for the domestics, who didn't have such privileges on their days off.

In fact Torfy didn't have to come herself. Mrs. Cox, a new auxiliary who worked part-time in Casualty at weekends, came up with the tray at half past nine. 'There aren't many jobs I can do yet,' she said. 'This is one I could manage.' She was plump and motherly. 'I'm used to looking after my own daughter. I made them give me a large pot of tea—I guessed you could do with it.'

There was one good thing about her—she didn't linger to gossip. When we'd first had auxiliaries to do odd-jobbing in the department Sister Lamont had practically torn out her hair by the roots because of their propensity for chat. 'There she is, rr-attl-ing away with the patients!' she would exclaim, as some white-overalled figure hovered uncertainly about the hall. 'Can she not be set to *scrr-ub* something?' In *her* training days, she said, there had been only two forms of life: probationers and qualified nurses. There had been something called 'assistant nurses' in places like cottage hospitals, but she had no experience of them. As for all these white overalls—with caps, auxiliaries; without, orderlies—she found it very difficult to fit them into the pattern. She seemed, however, to have accepted Mrs. Cox, largely because she was an enthusiastic tidier and had the sense to occupy herself without asking many questions. And possibly because she knew enough to make herself useful in the dressings section without putting her thumbs into sterile bowls, and was a neat bandager of other people's dressings.

It looked as if she had asked for double bacon and eggs, as well as a large pot of tea. That was just as well. If I managed to get through it I wouldn't need to get dressed and go over to the dining-room for lunch. I could potter, and wash my hair, and take a long bath, and go back to bed again ready for night-duty. If I didn't sleep, I could read. Torfy would see that I was up in plenty of time for night breakfast at eight-fifteen. Until then I could frankly laze. The prospect gave me far greater pleasure than any party could have done. If that was what Torfy meant by being anti-social I didn't see anything very reprehensible about it. We all had so very little time to be alone, to be idle in solitude. Surely, I thought, it was the insecure people who needed to be in a crowd? A regular ration of my own company was very precious to me, and that was something Torfy had never been able to understand.

Randall Brown was on late duty. When I reported he was clearing up after dealing with a minor accident, and there was still a policeman sitting at the CO's table copying names and addresses into his notebook.

'You clear off,' I told Randall. 'I'll finish this lot. Are you going to the party?'

He shook his curly head. 'No, ma'am, I am not. I'm going home to my wife and kids, quick sharp. But not till I leave it tidy for you.'

'Tripe,' I said. 'Go on, Randy. Or don't you trust me to do it properly?'

'Ah, if you put it like that...' He began to roll down his sleeves. 'Thanks, Clare. And turn this fellow out when he's done. No cups of tea.'

He was joking. 'Do I ever give policemen cups of tea?'

'Yes,' he said. 'Don't we all?'

As soon as he had gone I switched the kettle on. The police-man looked up. 'I didn't think we'd be seeing you on nights,

Nurse, now that you've passed your finals.'

'You may not see me on much more,' I said. 'This week I'm standing in for someone else.' I knew his face. I was waiting for his name to come to me. 'But I like nights; I always have.'

'I know.' He snapped the elastic band round his notebook and stuffed it into his top pocket again, 'I remember your saying so ... What happened to your friend? The dark one with the funny name?'

'Funny name?' I rinsed the pot with hot water and spooned tea into it from the tin labelled *Internal Use Only*. 'Oh, do you mean Nurse Bates? Torfy, we call her.'

'That's the one, yes.'

'She's here in Casualty, on days.'

'I must look out for her. My kid's always asking.'

It came then. The computer in my head clicked out the details. Torfy had nursed his son in the children's unit. I had admitted him. Field. The boy had been on a Robert Jones frame. Peter. Peter Field. 'Peter, wasn't it? How is he?'

'Oh, fine. We'll make a copper of him yet.'

I doubted that very much, but I didn't say so. 'Good,' I said. 'Help yourself to sugar. While you're here I'll just do my little trot round. See that there aren't any tramps kipping in the side-rooms or anything.'

'More likely to be hippies. I'll have dozens of them to move on when I go from here. They're squatting in those empty houses on the new bypass site—the ones for demolition. You wouldn't believe what a lot of people are soft enough to go taking them milk, and food, and so on. Paraffin stoves, even.'

I said: 'Why? Are they sorry for them? They *choose* to live that way, so I don't see why.'

'It makes me sick to see so many layabouts, when you girls work so hard. Look, *we* have to wash, keep ourselves respectable, don't we? Why can't they? Well, the Social Security people are wise to them now. No more public money if they don't toe the line. Quite right, too. Why should *we* keep them?'

'But that isn't the answer, is it? Don't you think that for

46

every genuine idealist, and for every calculating advantage-taker, there must be twenty who could be mentally ill?'

'Well, they've made themselves ill, with their drugs. Do you know—well, in your job I dare say you do—that the Midlands figures for mental illness are twice the national average? Makes you think, doesn't it?'

'Yes. But it could be a false figure. What it makes me think is that it's boosted by all the people who come here to get treated for drug addiction, and all the hippies who overflow here from London ... Pour yourself another cup, when you're ready. I won't be long.'

I went into every room, checked it, closed and locked the windows, and turned off the lights. Somebody had left the infra-red drier on in the plaster room, and it was like an oven in there. I opened all the windows, and locked the door on the hall side. In the orthoptic room there was a tap running, and some child had left a puddle on one of the small chairs near the synoptophore. Before I turned off the tap I washed and disinfected the chair, and washed my hands again. It was a good thing, I reflected, that some of us were made of sterner stuff than Miss Brackett's trainees in the squint clinic. One of them had once run helplessly to Sister Lamont to inform her that a small boy had vomited. She seemed to have no idea what to do about it, except to pass the buck to someone else. '*Really?*' Sister said interestedly. 'I wonder what the wee laddie can have been eating.' Then she walked away. History didn't relate who had finally cleaned up the mess, but it wouldn't have surprised me to hear that it was the night nurse, hours later.

When I had prowled round the rest of the rooms, the minor ops theatre, the recovery ward and the offices, and locked the door leading to the dispensary steps, I went back to P.C. Field. 'All clear,' I said. 'No tramps. No hippies. No fires or floods. Not even any patients.'

He looked up. 'No *patients*?' He frowned, not believing me. 'What about the chap in the recovery room?'

'What chap? You must be joking.'

'I'm not.' He pulled out his notebook again, and leafed

47

through it. 'Emery. James Emery, facial injuries. Admitted to casualty ward . . . It's in your big book too.'

'But I've been in there. There's not so much as a bed disturbed. Damn it, I put the light on for a moment.' Then I thought again. 'No, by golly, it *was* on. I turned it off.'

He got to his feet. 'Come on. I'd better help you to look for him . . . I know he's here, because I brought him up myself at eight o'clock, or just before. Before that cyclist came in.'

We found James Emery, neatly rolled in a blanket, lying peacefully asleep on the floor under one of the beds. He had slid out so gently that even the bedspread wasn't wrinkled. When we had lifted him back, still asleep, I said: 'If that's it, I'd better put cot sides on. Will you stay with him while I get them?'

I brought them from the storeroom one at a time, and we fixed them in position. Field said: 'Didn't Mr. Brown tell you he was here?'

'You know he didn't. You were there. But that's my own fault for hustling him out. And I'd have read it in the report book straight away if you hadn't been at the desk. Usually, you see, I read the book first, and *then* do my prowl round. I've done nights here before, and that's my routine. We all have our own habits.'

He put on his helmet and tapped it down in that final way that policemen have. 'Be on my way, then. Thanks for the tea, Nurse.'

'Think nothing of it,' I told him. 'Love to Peter.'

'Yes. And you tell Nurse Bates I was asking.'

I checked the casualty book, and found the Emery entry immediately above the one about a boy who had fallen from his bicycle, and then I went straight to the phone and rang Sister Duffy.

It is a very strict rule in any hospital that if a patient falls out of bed, or sustains any other injury, it must be reported at once both verbally and in writing. I said: 'Sister, I have one patient in the recovery ward, as you'll see from the bed-state. Facial injuries. I've just found him on the floor. He doesn't seem hurt, but perhaps someone should see him?'

'Have you put cot sides up?'

'Yes, Sister. He's sleeping now.'

She grunted, and muttered something about the residents being tied up, and then added: 'Well, if he *does* complain of anything, let me know. Can't be much wrong if he's sleeping.' She hung up before I could say any more, but that didn't matter. I had passed the responsibility to her, according to the rules, and I wasn't in the least worried about Emery. If I had been, I could have insisted on having First On to examine him.

I left just one small light on in the hall, at the top of the ramp by the entrance. We were on the same level as the rest of the hospital buildings, but a floor above the ambulance park. This meant that the glass-covered ramp descended from the hall to the ambulance entrance, and rose again to connect with the main block near the autoclave room. It was tough on the ambulance men, because they had to climb when their stretchers were occupied, and had an easy walk only when they were empty.

After I'd fixed the lights I went to sit in Sister's office, where I could hear anyone approaching up the ramp, and at the same time could listen out for Mr. Emery round the corner in the miniature ward. At least, I had planned to sit down, but I found that Sally Dane hadn't finished the cupboards after all, so I spent the next half hour or so finishing them, and putting away the things Randall Brown had used. In Casualty it is as well to get through chores early on, so as not to be caught napping. Sooner or later the ambulance bell would be ringing, if I knew my Saturday nights. Towards eleven, after the pubs were shut, and again just after twelve, when the Saturday dances finished.

Meanwhile it was very peaceful down there, away from the ward blocks with their constant background of small sounds, the occasional voice or the little clatter of crockery or stainless steel. I wondered why Matron thought three months' night duty in Casualty too long. I had done it twice, and I had spent most of the slack times revelling in the quietness, when I wasn't catching up on lecture notes. Some people found it lonely; a good many said that the old building was creepy at night, and kept lights burning everywhere, but it had never seemed to me other than a friendly place in the dark. Once I had run slap into the SSO in the hall, when all the lights were out, and he had been far more startled than I was.

I looked in on Mr. Emery a couple of times, and then sat down to read Sister's copy of *The Naked Ape*. She usually left her library books in the office for the night nurse, and I didn't know any other sister who would do that.

Torfy, I decided, had a good many neophobic gestures. So had my father. I didn't agree about left-handed mothers, though. Professor Morris seemed quite sure that they carried their babies on their left arms, automatically positioning them over the reassuring heartbeat. I was left-handed myself, I reflected, and so was my mother, and we held babies on our right arms. That made me wonder: was I perhaps insecure because Mother hadn't carried me the right way instinctively? Torfy would almost certainly say so. But if I was, why didn't the dark, rambling department scare me?

I was working that one out when I heard the first ambulance coming down the road. It was one of the new ones, with a kind of destroyer's siren instead of a bell. That meant it had come from the new station close to A5, and was almost certainly coming from a traffic accident.

I checked the doctors' rota list to see who was First On. It should have been Jim Kane, but his name had been crossed out and Leonora Kirk's substituted. Then I watched to see that the men were bringing a stretcher up the ramp before I rang through for her. One does. When the driver walks up alone there is no longer any hurry.

This time it wasn't too bad. It was a motor-cyclist, as I could have predicted. It seemed to us sometimes that nine out of ten road casualties were motor-cyclists— but probably we overestimated the numbers because we dreaded them so much. This one had been spared the terrible head injuries we saw so often: he was lucky. His face was scored with gravel burns, but his skull had escaped. He had a fractured humerus on one side, and a badly bruised arm and shoulder on the other which

50

was swollen so much that his leather jerkin was skin-tight. That is what a rider gets if he doesn't let go of his handlebars as he is thrown over them.

Miss Kirk, as broad as Toby Jarrett, loomed over him. She joined her thick black eyebrows in a straight bar and said: 'No helmet?' Her voice was as deep as a man's.

'Yes, I've got it here, Doctor,' the ambulance attendant said. 'I took it off in the ambulance, and his goggles.'

'Good.' She went on looking down at him. 'Because I'm not at all nice to damned fools who don't wear them! You hear, boy? ... Now, I want to look at these arms. Nurse will have to cut your jacket, but she'll try not to hurt you.'

He rolled his eyes at me when I brought the scissors. They looked doubly frantic because of the white rim left in the grime by his goggles. It wasn't wholly fear of pain, I knew. 'All right,' I told him. 'These leathers *are* expensive. I'll go along the seams as carefully as I can.'

Leonora Kirk made a kind of puffing noise that meant she thought me unnecessarily fussy. She didn't say anything, but she soon began tapping on the end of the couch with one finger, slowly and rhythmically. I reckoned it was about sixty-odd to the minute. I said: 'Professor Morris would have a word for that, Miss Kirk.' I had never found her as unapproachable as Torfy seemed to.

She stopped doing it. '*Touché*,' she said. 'One doesn't notice them oneself ... Have I any others, Miss Observant?'

I thought, while I nicked away at the seam of the jacket. I was wrecking the second-best stitch scissors, but I had been told often enough what leathers cost, and it horrified me. 'Yes. You tap your teeth with your pen when you're listening to a long spiel in OP. Especially if you don't believe a word of it, or if you're thinking about something more urgent that's waiting.'

'How well you know me already, Nurse ... Right, that's fine. Just support his forearm, will you?' She assessed the damage gently, listening for crepitus, extending the elbow very slowly. 'Look, we'll splint this temporarily with some of that do-it-yourself plastic nonsense. And he may as well have a

51

good old-fashioned lead and opium compress on the other—
you can't beat it. Then he can go in the recovery ward till
morning, and we'll have him X-rayed first thing. Right?'

I slid a look at the ambulance men, and they nodded their
willingness to wait and help me get the boy to bed. It wasn't
their job, but they were always very obliging about things like
that. 'Fine, Miss Kirk,' I said. While she kept the arm ex-
tended I got the rest of the jacket out of the way, and then the
grubby T-shirt, and fetched her the splinting.

It didn't take long, and the men soon had him in bed and
undressed for me. Before I left the ward I went across to look
at Mr. Emery. Sister Duffy had still not been down, or sent
anyone else to see him. It seemed to me I might as well ask
Leonora Kirk to take a look, just to be on the insured side.

It hadn't seemed important as I walked across the ward.
Suddenly it became urgent. I stayed beside him just long
enough to listen to one cycle of his altered breathing, and then
I ran.

She was still in the CO's room, filling in details of the
motor-cyclist in the book. I said: 'Can you come and look at
the other man I've got in? Facial injuries, but he's Cheyne-
Stokesing suddenly ... He fell out of bed earlier, there could
be a connection. Nobody's seen him since. I did report it.'

She came along at once. Together we listened to the gradu-
ally deepening, slowing respirations, and heard them fade
away again, and held our own breath during the silent hiatus
before the next build-up. She nodded. 'Better have him along
to Intensive straight away. You can't cope here. Ring and ask
them to send a bed trolley right away. Who admitted him?'

'Mr. Fiske, I think. Some time after eight.'

'It would be, yes. I didn't take over until ten. Get on that
phone right away, there's a good girl. What's his name?'

'Emery,' I said. 'James Emery.' Then I went to the office
telephone.

Half an hour later I had given the motor-cyclist the shot she
had written up for him, cleared the room up again, and seen
Emery off to the intensive care unit, with a porter and a junior
night nurse carrying a portable oxygen outfit to escort him.

Then I filled the kettle once more. This time the tea would be for me.

When it was made I carried it along to the office and settled down to the book again. I was beginning my second cup, and marvelling at the extraordinary quietness of the department on a Saturday night, when I heard footsteps coming up the ramp. Not very steady ones. I was used to that. Drunks were apt to wander in at night, just as tramps were. They seem to have some kind of homing device that leads them towards beds and shelter, and a hospital is the logical place when other refuges are closed for the night.

I prepared to carry out my tramp-scaring routine. The idea was to let them get well into the hall, and then startle them by switching on the big overhead lights all together. As often as not it meant that they took to their heels and didn't come back. I stood in the dark hall outside the office with my fingers on the main switches and waited ... When the visitor reached the small light at the top of the ramp I saw him clearly. Not an intruder after all, but Kenyon Fiske. I went back into the office and sat down again, putting the big table between me and the door, and carried on drinking my tea.

It took him quite a time to navigate his way along the hall, and he knocked over at least two chairs on the way. At last he reached the office, and stood swaying in the doorway, watching me. He was clearly well under the influence. His tie hung loose, his hair was a lank mess and his eyes were inclined to sideslip. It was not a pretty picture. 'Why'n't you come to party?' he demanded. 'Tol' you to come, di'n't I?'

I stood up. 'I'm on duty, Mr. Fiske.'

'Come to fesh you. Can't have party 'thout Snow Queen.' He laughed in a fatuous sort of way. 'Miss Frig-Frigidaire nine-sev'ty, thass you. C'm *on*.'

I should have stayed right where I was. I could have dodged him round that table all night and he could never have reached me. But Torfy was wrong: I was every bit as good at sticking my neck out as she was. Because I was angry I walked round the table, pushed him out into the hall, and said: 'Get out!' It was a stupid thing to do, because I'd learned long ago that the last part of a drunk's body to become powerless is his hands—and his came round my wrists as hard and sure as steel hand-cuffs.

'Got you now,' he said. 'C'm on, come party.'

I tried the old life-saver's trick of bringing both hands down forcibly against his thumbs. It had worked all right on fake-drowning Girl Guides, and even once on a genuinely drowning holidaymaker at Sheringham. It didn't work with Ken Fiske: it simply jerked his head down and forward so that he butted it into my shoulder. If I had then attempted the thigh-throw that Torfy and I had learned from a Judo-mad physiotherapist I should have thrown myself as well.

I stood quite still against the table, working out my next move. Meanwhile he forced my hands behind me and had his arms round my waist and his head boring into the side of my neck. I wanted to be sick. I still don't know why I didn't scream, except that it would have wasted energy and wouldn't really have helped. Possibly, too, I was remembering Jeremy's dictum that slaps were better than slating. At any rate, because the struggle was silent I was able to hear distinctly more foot-steps coming into the hall. At that moment I was busy calcu-lating ways of distracting Ken Fiske so that he would relax enough to enable me to get a knee between us and lever him off. Someone was coming. Someone who didn't know the lie of the land too well, and was sensibly feeling his way along the wall instead of blundering into chairs. I said: 'Let me *go*. There's somebody coming. Listen!' Then I managed to stamp hard on his instep: it was a manoeuvre the physio girl had warmly recommended for use with stiletto heels, but even with my flat ward shoes it was obviously effective, especially the preliminary side-scrape down the shin, because he yelped: 'Blast you!' and let me go so suddenly that I staggered back into the table. Then he reached out to knock off my cap with a contemptuous little backhanded flick. 'You 'n' your paper halo,' he said. 'Super—supercil's . . .' He gave that one up, and lurched out into the hall.

When I'd retrieved my cap from the table and put it on again I went to make sure that he had left the department, and to find out who else was there. There were two of them turning for the ramp: Ken Fiske was hanging on to the arm of a taller man whose back view I didn't recognise. A guest from the party, presumably, probably sent to collect the host. I listened to their footsteps fading away and then I poured myself another cup of tea and made myself drink it. I sat still until my pulse had cooled down to normal, and then I walked through into the dressings section and swabbed my face, neck, hands and forearms with *aether meth*. It stung, but I felt clean again. More or less. Torfy, I reflected, would have said I was being obsessive, but she hadn't been forced into close contact with Ken Fiske.

Towards one o'clock the ambulance siren sounded again. There were two stretchers this time. When I got through to the switchboard I asked: 'Is Miss Kirk still on call?'

'No, Nurse. The new CO took over as from midnight. Mr. Sargent, it is. What is it?' the porter asked.

After midnight they wanted details, so that residents weren't called from bed—if they had reached it—for minor things that Sister Duffy could take responsibility for. 'Car crash,' I told him. 'Driver abdominal injuries, passenger badly cut, both concussed. All right?'

'I'll get him right away, Nurse.'

'Thanks. Notify Sister, will you?' That was just a formality. I didn't expect her to come down. But there is a rule at most hospitals, and certainly at Fin's, that no night nurse may call out a resident directly: she may only approach him through the night super. The rule was relaxed for Casualty, but we were still required to notify her. Torfy said it was a dangerous and time-wasting rule, that originated in the days when it was considered 'fast' to address doctors directly. 'And "fast" is the same as "loose", oddly enough,' she had said. 'So you could let a patient die while you went through the channels, because it would be immodest to ring a man in his room.' All that would happen now would be that the porter would ring Sister Duffy, and say: 'CO to Casualty, Sister.' She would grunt, and get on with her meal, and that would be that. But if I hadn't notified her, and she had taken a random walk and found a resident in the department, it would have been pretty well a hanging offence. It was one of the professional traditions we could have done without. A lot of them seemed to be based on a theory that any male and female, left alone together, are bound to fall into sin. There was still a rule that a nurse alone with a doctor might not close the door of the room —and it applied whether the doctor happened to be male or female, and it had persisted since the days when female medicos didn't exist. It must all have been rather amusing for outsiders, but we didn't find it so. It was the kind of thing we had learned to live with.

I did what I could while I waited. I got the ambulance men to prop up the couch on high blocks and help me to undress the man, and then I removed the more obvious glass chips from the woman's face and folded clean gauze over the gashes. I didn't like the look of the man one bit. He was a ghastly colour, his skin was clammy and his pulse was faint and running.

When I heard the CO walk in I said straight away: 'This one first, Doctor! Internal haemorrhage.' Then I turned round. He had grey eyes, broad shoulders and thick brown hair, and it was a quick pain, a lurch of the diaphragm, to see him. 'Neil,' I said.

For perhaps ten seconds we stood staring at one another, then we snapped out of it and got on with our work. He took blood for matching, and shot the man along to Intensive immediately, without any prodding around. 'You chaps take him,' he said. 'No time for red tape.' Then he looked quickly at the woman. 'Yes. Get cleaning and stitching,' he told me. 'I want to fix this blood. You can suture the scalp; leave the face for me.' He went running full belt down the ramp as I reached for the forceps.

I had the scalp wounds cropped, cleaned and stitched by the time he came back, and half a dozen small skin needles threaded with our finest sutures ready for him. I hung up his coat while he scrubbed, and he carried on where I had left off. He looked at my stitches first. 'Nice work,' he said. 'Thanks, Nurse.' He was on the job: I was 'Nurse' now, and not Clare, and I understood that.

He closed the long gashes in her cheeks with delicate small stitches that would leave scarcely any scars. It took a long time. Afterwards he examined her completely, but there didn't seem to be any other injury apart from a great blue bruise on her forehead and another on one thigh. 'Right,' he said. 'She can go to an ordinary ward, I think. Who takes in tonight?'

'It's this morning now,' I told him. 'So it'll be Mr. Dersingham.'

'Ring 'em, will you? Say I'm sending her up.'

'Yes. They'll have to fetch her. I've no night porter, and the ambulance men have gone—and anyway, they're not supposed to do it—and I can't leave the department.' It didn't occur to me until then that I hadn't been relieved for Meal. Not that it mattered. I wasn't hungry.

'Fix it, then. What's the documentation here for admissions?'

I shoved him the book, and the slips that had to go to the wards and the records office, and gave him the slip the ambulance men had left. Then I rang S5F, and waited to hand the patient over to their junior. After I had seen her off down the ramp with her trolley I went back to the CO's room. Now perhaps we could talk.

He sat on the corner of the desk, drying his hands, and I went to take the towel from him. Then I brought his white coat, which was stiff and new, and helped him into it. At last he sat down again. He was frowning faintly. 'You say you can't leave the department. Not even for a meal?'

'Oh, they send me a relief for half an hour or so, for that ... Neil, are you just a locum, or have you——'

His face cleared. 'I see. So you weren't here when I came down earlier?'

'When you—— But I must have been. Nobody's relieved me yet. I think Sister must have forgotten me.'

'I see.' He got up and braced his shoulders as if he had driven a car a long way and was very tired. 'So you *were* here.' He walked over to the window and stood peering down into the ambulance park. 'I mean when Mr. Fiske was here.'

'Was it you—who came and took him away?'

He kept his back towards me. 'That was a pretty squalid little scene, wasn't it?'

I stared at the wide shoulders, at the way his hair grew to a point at the neck, and I was stung by the bite of criticism in his voice. 'It wasn't of *my* making,' I said defensively. 'You don't know how glad I was to hear someone coming. I thought I'd never get him to go.'

He shrugged then, and walked towards the door without looking at me. 'Thank you, Nurse,' he said.

'Neil, *you* saw the state he was in! Do you seriously think I gave him any encouragement?'

'I don't know,' he said very quietly. 'And I'm not particularly interested. Goodnight, Nurse.' He closed the door behind him.

I stood there trembling for a long time before I felt I could trust my legs to take me back to the office. It was ten minutes more before I could control my voice on the phone. Then I rang the switch man again. 'Nobody's relieved me for a meal,' I told him. 'It's too late now, but perhaps you can find out what went wrong?'

'Hold on, Nurse,' he said. 'Sister Duffy's here beside me. I'll ask.' When he came back on the line I could tell from his voice that she was still there, leaning into his window hatch to listen. 'It's like this, Nurse. Casualty are making their own night-duty arrangements now, Sister says. Sister Lamont hasn't asked her for a night relief, and she can't spare anybody now.'

'But that's absurd!' I said. 'What are we supposed to do— bring sandwiches on with us? And where would we get them?' All the hysteria I had bottled up since Neil walked out was bubbling to the surface. 'Ask her that,' I went on. 'No, don't. Leave it, Thomas.'

'Er, Nurse ... Sister says she'll see if there's——'

'Tell her not to bother,' I said. 'I've got the doctors' biscuits, thank you. I shan't starve.'

Then I put the phone down and went and checked on the motor-cyclist again. When I'd made sure he was sleeping, and that his pulse was satisfactory, I let myself sit down and cry all over Sister Lamont's big green blotter. That didn't help either.

CHAPTER 4

CATHY WEAVER took over from me next morning. She was fighting back a yawn as she came in. 'Some party,' she said. 'Don't residents *ever* sleep? Much happen down here?'

I could have written a volume about that, but it wouldn't have been what she meant. 'Very quiet,' I told her. 'Only three casualties. Pretty slack for a Saturday.'

She was looking through the entries in the book. 'Oh? N. J. Sargent. So you've met the new CO, have you? I wonder what "N" stands for—I didn't get his first name at the party. He only popped in briefly.'

'It's Neil,' I said. When she looked up, surprised, I added: 'When *I* met him I didn't get his surname. Last year's Rag ball. One of Torfy's string of brothers knows him—Mick, I think.'

'I see! Then you'll be able to gen us all up. Well? Is he or isn't he?'

'Is he what?'

'Oh, be your age, Kennedy. Is he married, engaged or otherwise involved?'

'I've no idea.' That was a question I hadn't even asked myself, and it was a jolt to realise it. To me he had appeared as an isolated person, without background. I told her and myself: 'At his age he's surely committed. He's over thirty, and he's hardly the kind girls don't notice.' That was cold fact.

'Isn't it always the way?' Cathy let out an exaggerated sigh. 'We get rid of a little tick like Ken Fiske, who couldn't give himself away with a quarter of tea, and get a replacement who looks like every girl's dream come true—and then we find he's booked ... Still, I gather he's living in, so you could be wrong.'

'I told you,' I reminded her, 'I don't *know*. I was only surmising.' Married residents had been known before—but only on a temporary basis. Perhaps he was only with us for a short time?

'But you're probably right, Kennedy. It sounds reasonable ... Well now. The humerus man—he's for X-ray first thing?'

'Yes. The chit's on the table there. Miss Kirk signed it last night. And Emery's gone to IC. Oh, but he was admitted after you went off. Randy knows about him.'

'I suppose he's why the SSO had to keep dashing up there last night, is he?'

I nodded. 'Could be. But we sent him an abdominal crush, too, that was pretty dicey.'

'Hm. They lost one, I know.'

That didn't surprise me at all. If the car driver had much more than the ruptured spleen I had suspected it would take more than Humphrey Sumner and his beloved unit to do very much about it. 'Bad luck,' I said. 'Look, will you tell Sister that I got no Meal relief last night, and that Sister Duffy was rather more than obstructive about it? Casualty are "making their own arrangements", she says. She's just not going to lay on any relief unless Sister Lamont *asks* for it. I had to subsist on departmental biscuits last night, so you'll need to get more for the CO's elevenses.'

I didn't bother to go to night nurses' dinner. For one thing I was past wanting it; for another, if Sister Duffy wanted to disown Casualty mealwise, I told myself, she couldn't very well claim the right to compel me to eat a stodgy three-course dinner on such a warm October morning.

It was a long time before I got to sleep, and when the corridor maid called me at half past seven I was still heavy and confused. I was last in to breakfast, and Sister Duffy didn't miss the fact. Afterwards, as we collected our bags and capes from the shelf outside the dining-room, she tapped me on the shoulder. 'If you're sufficiently awake to listen, Nurse Kennedy...'

'Yes, Sister?'

'You'll be relieved for Meal when I have a runner free. I can't say what time, but I can't help that.'

'Thank you, Sister,' I said. I doubt if I sounded very grateful.

'And tomorrow morning you'll kindly put in an appearance at dinner, like anyone else. You Casualty people may think you're a law unto yourselves, but I don't think Matron would agree.'

In other words, if I didn't show up at dinner she would report me to Miss Macintosh. If she did, I reflected, it would at least bring the relief question to a head. But I said: 'Very well, Sister.' The quickest way to silence Sister Duffy was, as we all knew, to agree with her.

There was a flap on in Casualty when I arrived, or the aftermath of one. There were a couple of flat-capped policemen and two or three other people out in the hall. Cathy Weaver was still on duty, and so was Johnny Winter, as well as Torfy, who was legitimately late nurse. I dumped my cape in the office and went straight through to the dressings section. Cathy was just finishing off a head bandage for a long-haired youth with tears rolling down his face; Johnny and Janey Watts were working on another boy's arm, and in the end cubicle Torfy was sorting out bits of glass and road dirt from the forehead of a yellow-frizzed girl lying on the couch. The girl was crying too.

I said: 'What can I do?'

'Nothing here,' Torfy told me. 'I'm just waiting for the CHS to take a look at this.'

'Buzz off,' I said. 'I'll scrub up and look after it.'

She shook her head. 'The other two should have gone off at six. I'll see this one through now. Shove Cathy Weaver off.'

'Yes, I will. I think she's about finished ... Just what was all this?' I followed Torfy across to the sink. 'Two cars?'

'An articulated truck, and a Hillman Imp. *Seven* of them in it! One's gone to Intensive, three were b.i.d.' She went back to

61

her stool and carried on picking out glass and grit with her dissecting forceps, and tinkling them into the kidney-dish on the pillow.

The girl began to sob. 'Where are the others? Where *are* they?' she kept saying. 'They're dead, aren't they? Why don't you tell me? Nurse, where's *Geoff*?'

Without looking at me Torfy pointed to her own third finger and then turned down a thumb behind the girl's head. Geoff, I took it was—had been—her fiancé. That was how it was with road accidents. People, situations, were wiped out in catastrophic seconds of time. We were supposed to get used to it, but I never did. The quick waste was quite different from ward deaths after illnesses.

'Hush, love,' Torfy said. 'Doctor won't be long now.' I noticed the flashy engagement ring as I walked out.

I found Cathy Weaver in the office with Janey Watts. They both looked fed up to the teeth. 'You missed all the fun,' Cathy told me. 'God, what an evening we've had! Three of this lot b.i.d. Before that we had three separate crashes, all after half past five. Every time we cleared up another lot came in. I still haven't seen this lot's relatives—the police have chased some parents up, I think ... Can you cope, Kennedy?'

'Of course I can. Did you certify, Miss Watts?'

She nodded. 'I'll see them too. Poor souls. The one kid—the girl—was only fifteen. The driver was seventeen, and drunk. According to him they were all high on amphetamines —the girl Sheila had bought them at *school*, if you please!'

Cathy lifted an eyebrow. 'Fillimore Secondary Modern again, was it? And there's the Head bleating in the local rag about how such things *never* happen in *his* school.'

'Wishful thinking,' Janey said. 'Seven of them in an Imp, no chance to manoeuvre at speed; what did they expect? And there may be more before the night's out. There's a bad patch of oil somewhere. A tanker overturned.'

I asked: 'Aren't the police doing anything about it?' I meant the school, rather than the tanker, but Cathy took it I meant the oil.

'They're trying. But there's so much traffic on A5 at this

time on a Sunday. People belting back from Welsh weekends and so on—and they simply won't stop for police or anyone else. They go blinding on ... They've had one policeman knocked down already. They never learn, do they? ... Well, I'm off. Chuck Johnny out soon, and Bates.'

'Oh lord, Nurse Bates is waiting for me,' Janey remembered. 'I'd better see that girl before we talk to the relatives.' She turned to me. 'Can you lay on some tea for them while I carry on?'

'Surely,' I said. 'I expect you could use some too.'

I glanced out into the hall counting heads. There were fewer now. Three women and a man. They all looked grey and stunned. One of the women was crying, and a tall patrol-car driver stood with his arm round her shoulders, rocking her gently. The heartbeat rhythm again, I thought. Professor Morris would have been interested in that, but maybe not as moved by it as I was because he had studied it oftener.

When the tea was ready I carried the tray along the hall and set it on a chair near the sad little group. 'I've brought you some tea,' I said distinctly. People who are shocked have difficulty in taking things in unless you raise your voice a little and speak slowly. 'I want you to drink it now, and then you can see the doctor ... Take all the sugar you want. It'll help.'

One by one I put the cups into their hands and stirred in the sugar for them. I left the saucers on the tray: they had enough to cope with, to hold the cups steady. One by one they stared uncomprehendingly at the tea and then drank. The woman next to the policeman kept saying, over and over again: 'What was she *doing* with these people? What was she *doing* in the car?'

'Steady, love,' I said. 'Doctor won't be long.' Not that Janey Watts was going to be able to tell her very much, but doctor-won't-be-long always comforts them. Just as Sister-wants-a-word-with-you used to frighten them, so that we learned to transpose it to wouldn't-you-like-to-talk-to-Sister?

I put two cups where the policemen could reach them, and took Janey hers in the CO's room. Then I threw Johnny Winter out and began on the clearing up.

63

By ten o'clock Torfy had gone, the walking cases and their relatives had been sent home, and the yellow-headed girl to S5F. Janey Watts was still filling in forms, and the two police-men were with me, trying to persuade the dead girl's mother to go home. We weren't having much success. 'Look, Mrs. Rogers,' I said, 'I'm sure the officer will gladly drive you home, and help you to explain to your husband. Or would you like him to fetch your husband for you? He'll be home by now, surely?' We all knew by now about his darts match at the Red Lion, and the fact that he never missed *News at Ten* on tele-vision.

'I want to see the *doctor*,' she said yet again. 'Not that bit of a girl, in there. A *proper* doctor.'

There was no future in explaining all over again that Janey Watts was as proper a doctor as she was ever likely to see. I'd tried, and it hadn't worked. What she wanted, I knew—though she hadn't said so—was to see a *male* doctor. 'You'd better go, boys,' I told the policemen. 'I expect you go off patrol at ten, don't you? In theory. I'll look after her—and thanks for all your help.'

The observer went on ahead, and I walked as far as the door with the driver. He said: 'Let's hope he's in better condition today ... Your "proper" doctor, I mean. Boy, was he loaded yesterday evening!'

They had evidently heard about Kenyon Fiske. 'That one's left,' I said. 'Or I should think he has by now. That's what he was celebrating.'

'Oh well. One excuse is as good as another, I suppose.'

'For heaven's sake don't broadcast it,' I said. 'We don't want the public to get the idea that Fin's men normally get into *that* state! After all, it was an occasion. And honestly, I've never known him do it before. Or anyone else, either ... Goodnight now. I must see to Mrs. Rogers.'

I went in to Janey and closed the door. 'Mrs. Rogers,' I said. 'I've not yet got round to telling her about the inquest, any more than you did. And I can't get her to go home, and she's asking to see "a proper doctor". Meaning, I take it, one of the men. Sorry, but I think we're lumbered until she does.

64

She ought to have a sedative, poor dear, but she just isn't going to accept it from mere females like you and me. Well, you heard how she talked to you ... Would it hurt your pride?'

Janey smiled in a crooked sort of way. 'I'm used to it. Yes, I'll ask a real live he-man to oblige. I'm going up to the common-room now, and I'll brief one of them. What's the girl's name again?'

'Sheila,' I said. 'Sheila Rogers.'

She wrote it on the back of her hand. It was a habit she had, just as we wrote things on the turned-up corners of our aprons. I often wondered whether notes like: *Smith, b.n.o. Apt,* or: *? d.o. Fri.* intrigued the laundry women. 'I come into my own,' Janey said, 'when they get people who won't let them do p.v.s and they have to get me instead. It cancels out.'

'Yes,' I said, 'I suppose so ... You haven't told Mum about the purple hearts, have you?'

'No. No point at this stage. I dare say it'll come out at the inquest, but we can shield her from the seamy side for one night, at least, poor woman.'

'Good,' I said. 'All right, I'll get her another cuppa while you chase somebody up. A proper doctor. I'll have a shot ready for him to give her. Pethidine?'

'Yes, I think so. It'll relax her, and she must have a raging head by now. Not that anyone else would use it in the circumstances, but I think that sort of shock merits it.' She got up to go. 'Fifty milligrams. Then she can go home and maybe sleep.'

'Right,' I said. 'Thank you very much, Miss Watts.'

About three minutes after she'd gone Neil Sargent came striding silently into the department. He had spared no effort to show that he was 'a proper doctor'. Not only was he wearing a freshly unfolded white coat, but he also had an unaccustomed stethoscope dangling from the pocket. It was Toby Jarrett's: I could see the initials T.M.J. that Toby had punched out with Sister Lamont's Dymo gadget. When I walked to meet him he said: 'This Mrs. Rogers?'

'That's right ... This is Dr. Sargent,' I told her, before I melted into the background. In the department every surgeon, physician and even final-year student on occasion is called 'Doctor' in public earshot. Otherwise patients suspect that 'Mister' may be merely a lab assistant, or even a porter, and not 'a proper doctor'. They are confused by so many white coats, and unable to spot the differences between them as we can. If Mrs. Rogers wouldn't accept Janey Watts it was highly unlikely that she would put her trust in anyone called 'Mr. Sargent', with or without a stethoscope.

As soon as he had sat down beside her I went into the office, but I could still hear every word in the quiet building. He said gently: 'I'm so very sorry about Sheila, Mrs. Rogers. You've had a very nasty shock, and I know how brave you've been. I want you to go on being a brave woman, because it won't be easy for you to tell your husband, I know. Try to be calm for his sake. In a moment I'm going to give you something to help you.' I took the hypodermic tray to him and watched him slip the needle neatly into her forearm as he went on talking. When he dropped the swab into the receiver I left them again. 'You understand that there has to be an inquest on these young people? It's just a formality, but it's the law, you see. There's no need for you to attend unless you wish. Do you understand?'

'Yes, Doctor.' She began to cry again. 'But what was she *doing* in this car? I don't understand.'

'That will sort itself out when the police have talked to the other youngsters. Put it aside for tonight, my dear ... Now, will you let me drive you home?'

That was absolutely unheard-of. I had never known the most junior houseman involve himself so far in a patient's private life. And it was quite unnecessary. I walked out to them. 'Doctor, I can get a sitting car, if——'

He stood up, lifted her to her feet, and put an arm protectively round her shoulders. 'Thank you, Nurse. I'm off duty and perfectly free to go. I think Mrs. Rogers would like me to see her husband.' He didn't look me in the face. 'Come along my dear. Let's get you home to your bed.'

She went with him obediently, a little unsteadily, mopping her eyes as she went. They must have passed Jeremy Gibbon somewhere along the ramp, because he came into the hall almost immediately and said: 'Well, now I've seen everything!'

'Yes. He's very kind,' I said. 'She wouldn't let the police take her.'

Jeremy stopped laughing. 'What's the score?'

'Her only daughter—just fifteen—killed outright in a car with a lot of youngsters Mum didn't know. The usual story. Janey says they were all full of amphetamines. Mrs. Rogers's little innocent had been dishing them out. She hasn't told the mother—she had enough to face up to for one night ... And what can I do for you at this hour?'

'You can unlock the dispensary door for me, my lovely. The SMO's got our key, and I can't locate him. Chatting up *la* Macintosh, I wouldn't wonder. I'll bet she's a better chess player than dear old Tetlow.'

I had locked the doors while Janey had talked to Mrs. Rogers, but I still had the keys in my pocket. 'And how do I know that your visit's legitimate?'

'You don't, ducky. I could be going to stuff myself silly with hard drugs. Or I could filch enormous quantities to flog round the coffee bars ... No, you don't believe a word, do you? Well, actually, I want some Parentrovite to shoot into our erstwhile CO.'

'Ken Fiske?' I said. 'I thought he'd gone.'

'Alas, no. He's lying on his little bed with the hangover to end all hangovers. The only thing to do is to give him a ginormous shot of the well-known instant soberiser, I fear. Otherwise we're never going to get rid of him, and that will never do, will it?'

It was wonderful what vitamin B would do, I said, and added: 'All right, you've convinced me. Here's the key. And use a blunt needle, for me. I'm still wild with him.'

'Oh?' Jeremy put his head on one side and waited.

'He came down here last night ...'

'Aha! And assailed your maiden virtue, no doubt.'

'Why do you say that?'

'Well, he did mention in his cups that he proposed to do

something of the kind. But I thought our friend Sargent had deflected him from his fell purpose, as it were. He certainly promised to do some rather unpleasant things to him if he did.'

I wondered. 'Did Mr. Sargent hear Ken mention me by name?' Had he done that for me, or for some unknown Casualty nurse? It was absurd how much it mattered.

Jeremy scratched his head and put on a thinking face. 'No. Only as that touch-me-not something-or-other whatsit down in Cas, I think.'

'But how did Ken know I was on nights?'

'Oh, because Torfy presented your apologies and said you'd been shoved on nights ... Anyhow, old sobersides jumped on him with both large feet, so I didn't imagine you'd need a bodyguard, old dear.'

'No. I had one, though.'

'You did?'

'Old sobersides, as you call him. He thought it was "a squalid little scene". So it was—but *I* didn't precipitate it, whatever your definition of a lady may be.'

Jeremy sighed. 'Oh dear, oh dear. I do see your problem. Never mind, time will tell, and all that jazz. He will discover in the fulness thereof what a virtuous little type you really are. Not to worry ... Well, I'd better get this healing draught, I think.'

'Don't forget the blunt needle,' I reminded him. 'And bring that key back!'

I went to tidy the CO's room then. When Jeremy came back with his box of ampoules I was checking the death certificate book. It was always kept there: collecting relatives were invariably directed to OP, so that they didn't have the traumatic experience of visiting a ward with a significant empty bed, or, worse, a ward with a stranger installed in the bed they had sat beside.

I asked him whether he knew which of Saturday's patients Intensive had lost. He said he hadn't a clue. 'But I know the SSO was a mite put out about it, whichever. Muttering darkly about "it never should have happened" and so forth. Why?'

'Oh, no reason, really. Just that we never do know, down here, what happens in the next chapter. Same as theatre. I have a sneaking urge to follow them up. I get interested.'

He wagged his finger at me. 'Cardinal sin, that is. It's known as "getting involved". Doesn't do, young Kennedy. No, it's not on, and you know it.'

'Well, just what do you think the CO is doing right now? Isn't he involving himself?'

'I've come to the conclusion, during our brief acquaintance-ship, that that one is a law unto himself. But there, he's big enough and ugly enough to make his own decisions. You, on the other hand, are a mere child of twenty-one or so, and you're supposed to toe the impersonal line. See?' He looked back from the door to ask: 'By the way, how d'you like the new matron-piece?'

I said I'd merely caught sight of her back view, and that I didn't really expect to encounter her until I went back to days.

I had spoken too soon. At seven o'clock in the morning Sister Duffy came down to the department looking as savage as I'd ever seen her. She took me into the office and closed the door, and folded her arms ominously. With her that was an aggressive posture, even if Professor Morris would diagnose it as self-protection. 'Now, Nurse Kennedy. Saturday night. Throw your mind back, if you please.'

'Yes, Sister?' It struck me suddenly that maybe she *was* windy, rather than angry, and didn't mean to admit it. Her image was that of the hard nut to crack, and she wasn't going to abandon it lightly.

'Emery. A man named James Emery. Well? What can you tell me about him?'

'Only that he was admitted to the recovery ward before I came on, Sister. Then later he deteriorated—he came up with Cheyne-Stokes breathing—and Miss Kirk transferred him to IC.'

'He fell out of bed, didn't he?'

'Fell, or climbed, yes. I did report it, Sister.'

She brushed that aside. '*Why* did he fall out?'

I spread my hands and shrugged. I couldn't say that it was because Randall Brown hadn't put up cot sides. 'I don't know, Sister.'

'Don't you?' Her eyes were like small currants in her grey-beige face. It occurred to me that she must be hypermetropic. 'I'll remind you, Nurse, that it happened while you were on duty. You were responsible for him.'

Again I had to be careful. It could have happened before I arrived. It seemed safest to say: 'Yes, Sister.'

'You know that he died?'

'No, I didn't!' Then it had not been the car driver, after all? I was glad that he at least was alive and fighting. He had looked a nice little man. 'I hadn't heard, Sister.'

'Well, he did. And there's been a post-mortem. As a result there's to be an enquiry ... Kindly present yourself at Matron's office at ten o'clock this morning. Understand?'

'Yes, Sister.' I wondered whether she would be there too. If I was responsible, so was she as my immediate superior. And would Randall Brown be called? 'What was the cause of death, Sister?'

'What do you think it was?'

The man had apparently been booted in the face. It could be that his skull had taken more of the jar than we knew. 'A cerebral accident, Sister?' Only somehow that didn't ring true. The breathing wasn't right—unless, of course, his respiratory centre had been directly damaged. 'Was it?'

'It could have been precipitated by the fall. The fall out of bed,' she said slowly.

'But, Sister, he came *in* with head injuries. They could have been more extensive than they seemed.'

'According to Mr. Fiske they were all facial and frontal. They found one that was occipital at the p.m., Nurse. According to the pathologist there was an extensive haemorrhage under it. And there's nothing to say it occurred at the same time as the others.'

'Oh *no*,' I said softly.

'Oh *yes*, Nurse. I'm sure you see the implications. You know what the relatives are going to say, don't you?'

70

I nodded miserably. 'Negligence, Sister.'

'*Your* negligence, Nurse Kennedy?'

'I—I don't know. I just don't *know*, Sister.'

'Then you'd better think about it before you go to the office, hadn't you?'

'Very well, Sister, I'll be there at ten.'

Before the others came on I had time to check the casualty book. I should be asked what time I found Emery on the floor, and what time Miss Kirk had seen him. *Found on floor, 9.30,* I read. *Seen by Miss Kirk 11.35, trans. ICU 11.45.*

Nine-thirty. Half an hour had gone by before I even knew that James Emery existed. And it *was* my fault. I should have looked at the book before I did anything else, whether or not Randall Brown had reported verbally, and whether or not the policeman had sat with his papers and notebook scattered over the book. A verbal report meant nothing: it was merely a bonus, extra to the written word. The book was what mattered —we'd had that drilled into us often enough. Whatever happened to a patient, or was administered to him, must be recorded in *writing*. The person in charge of a ward or department must hand over with a *written* report. I hadn't been at Fin's for more than three years without knowing all about that.

Randall didn't arrive with the others. 'He's doing the late turn instead of me,' Johnny Winter explained. 'Anything important?'

'No. Doesn't matter. Why did you swop?'

'His offer, not mine. A morning date, perhaps?'

So Randall knew about the enquiry. He had known the previous night. So how was it that Sister Duffy hadn't? Perhaps Matron hadn't told her until she had her morning tea. It was customary at St. Finbar's for the night super to take Matron's morning tea to her flat, and report in person, instead of handing over to an Assistant at eight o'clock. Miss Tetlow had always had hers at seven-fifteen. Evidently Miss Macintosh was an earlier bird.

I managed to corner Torfy in the CO's room before I went off. I said: 'Maybe Randy's told you about this enquiry?'

She frowned. 'What enquiry?'

'Isn't that why he swopped for the late duty?'

She looked at me blankly. 'I don't know what you're babbling about, but the only reason I know for Randy staying late today is that he promised Johnny last night that he would—so that Johnny wasn't late two nights in succession through staying on for that crash. Randy would have stayed last night, but he couldn't because his wife wanted him to baby-sit while she went to see their GP.'

That simple explanation hadn't occurred to me. So maybe he didn't know, after all. I gave Torfy the gist as quickly as I could. 'I feel awful,' I said.

Torfy was optimistic. It wasn't her trouble. 'Well, Neil Sargent isn't going to let them pin anything on *you*, is he? I saw brother Mick on Sunday morning, and he says Neil was fishing to find out whether you were still here, and so on, before he came.'

So Neil *had* known I was in Casualty when he'd tried to stop Ken Fiske coming down. 'This week's funny story,' I said. 'We're not even on speaking terms. He thinks I'm always having to be rescued from men, I think.'

'So? I always think jealousy's a nice healthy sign, in moderation. Good luck at the enquiry, anyhow.'

The last time I'd been to a Matron's enquiry had been when I was working in theatre. There had been a swab missing on the count; I'd reported one light, but Mr. Crockett—who was the SSO's holiday locum—had failed to locate it and had insisted that we must have been one short in the original bundle. None of us had believed that, because of all the double checking that went on when they were put in the drums, and when they were laid out, but Mr. Crockett had closed up just the same. Subsequently the patient had developed a general peritonitis; they had opened up and the missing swab had been found. Miss Tetlow had had the entire theatre staff, and the SSO and the senior HS, in her office to discuss whether we needed to change the checking system.

This time it wasn't like that. In the outer office Miss Corfield, the secretary, said: 'Mr. Brown's in now. You're next,

Nurse. Sit down, will you?'

After a while Randy came out, and Miss Corfield nodded to me to go in. As I passed him I murmured: 'Wait for me.' He nodded, but he didn't smile. He looked pretty anxious. Then I took a deep breath and walked in.

The office was different already. For one thing the desk was clear. Instead of Miss Tetlow's clutter of letter baskets and folders, and stationery racks and scribbling pads, Miss Macintosh had nothing but a small reminder pad, an ashtray and a bowl of enormous incurled bronze chrysanthemums. It was the first time I'd seen the desk so well-polished too. She sat there looking up at me, waved me to a chair—which was unprecedented—and then consulted her pad momentarily. 'Ah, yes. It's Nurse Kennedy?'

'Yes, Matron. Casualty nights.'

'I want to ask you one or two questions, Nurse, about Mr. James Emery, a patient who was admitted from Casualty by the Intensive Care Unit on Saturday night.'

'Yes, Matron.' Her voice was light and friendly, but that didn't necessarily mean very much.

'Tell me, please, exactly where you entered the picture. Take your time.' She folded her hands on the edge of the desk and waited. She had none of Miss Tetlow's fidgets.

'I went on duty at nine, Matron. Mr. Brown was clearing up and there was a policeman there making some notes. I persuaded Mr. Brown to go off, and to leave the clearing to me. You see, if he misses the nine-ten bus——'

'Yes, I understand. He explained that.' She leaned forward a little. 'Did he tell you about Mr. Emery?'

I had to think quickly. If I said he hadn't he could just be in trouble. And I had no idea what he had told her. And Randy had a wife and children, and his job was important to him. 'Oh, it was in the book, Matron.'

'I know, Nurse. But did he *tell* you about him?'

There was no rule which said he had to. 'Oh, he must have done, Matron. I can't remember exactly *what* he said, but he would naturally mention it.' I hurried on past the danger point. 'At any rate, when I went to look at him I found him on

73

the floor, under the bed.'

'At half past nine, I see. What were you doing until then, Nurse?' Her big brown bush-baby eyes didn't appear to blink at all. It was disconcerting.

'I—well, I did a round of the department, turning off lights and locking windows, and so on, checking all the rooms.'

'You always do that first?'

I begged the question. 'People sometimes get in; we get tramps sometimes, looking for somewhere to sleep. And sometimes there are taps left on, or lights burning, and——'

'Yes, Nurse, I see *why* you do it. I asked you whether you always do that *first*. Before you look at your patients?'

'Not—not usually, no.' There was no point in evading the issue.

'And were you by any chance chatting with the policeman you mentioned, instead of getting on with your work?'

I tried to remember what we had said. Very little, I thought. 'He did mention his son—he's an ex-patient, Matron. I think that was about all. Oh, and I gave him a cup of tea, but that was really to get him to stay there while I did my round. In case I didn't hear someone come in, I mean.'

She made a note of some kind with her red pen. 'Nurse, I want you to think carefully. When you did this—this reconnaissance of yours, you did include the recovery ward?'

There was a catch somewhere, but I could not quite see it. Torfy would have done. 'Oh yes, Matron. When I get to that end I do Minor Ops, recovery ward, orthoptics and then lock the door to the dispensary stairs.'

'I see. And you did lock that door?'

'Oh yes.'

'And you hadn't seen the patient then?'

I walked right into it. 'Well, no—I mean he was on the floor, so I couldn't.'

'Of course not, Nurse.' Her voice was silky. 'You didn't miss him because you didn't know he was there, did you?'

I had dropped Randy right into it, and I wanted to kick myself. I burst out: 'Mr. Brown wasn't *obliged* to tell me, Matron. It was all in the book. The reason I didn't know was

74

because I hadn't disturbed the policeman to look at the book, not because I hadn't been told.'

She smiled faintly at my vehemence. 'Nobody is blaming Mr. Brown, Nurse. Dear me, this is the nine-ten bus over again, isn't it? As you say, he was not obliged to report verbally. And if you hustled him out it's not surprising that he didn't, is it? ... Well, when you did find Mr. Emery, what then?'

'The policeman helped me to get him back into bed. He was a big man.'

'And then?'

I wondered whether Sister Duffy had admitted that I'd reported it, or not. 'Then I put cot sides up at once, Matron.'

'Quite right. And?'

There was no help for it. 'Then I rang Sister Duffy.'

'But nobody came to see the man?'

'Miss Kirk saw him, when she came to do an admission.'

'Two hours later?' She made it sound like a year.

'Yes, Matron.'

'Did you ask her to see him? Or did Sister Duffy?'

'Well, I did. But I dare say Sister Duffy had mentioned it to her as well.' If a cockerel had crowed it would not have surprised me. 'I was worried because he began Cheyne-Stokes breathing.'

'Yes, I'm sure you were, Nurse. Well, I think that's all. I merely wanted to establish whether there had been any negligence on the part of the hospital. I think the picture is clear enough now. Thank you, Nurse.'

She was waiting for me to go. She hadn't said whether she thought I'd been negligent or not, and there was nothing in her face or her manner to tell me. I said: 'Matron, *is* it my fault he—that they lost him?'

'Do you think it is, Nurse?'

'To be honest, no. Because I don't think the fall hurt him at all. He'd sort of slid out gently. And it was a low bed. Besides—— Well, I don't think he did die of head injuries at all.'

Her eyebrows were exactly like Elizabeth Taylor's. In fact

75

she was fairly Taylorish altogether. She opened her eyes wide and said: 'Don't you? Well, the post-mortem isn't completed yet, so you may prove to be right, Nurse. Run along now, thank you.' When I got to the door she said: 'Nurse, don't worry too much about this. But do be a little more careful in future.'

I said: 'Yes, Matron.'

Randy was waiting in the corridor outside. He said: 'I didn't know what to say to her. Look, Clare, Ken Fiske was so tight he couldn't have examined a sick cat. He didn't examine Emery at all. He didn't do one tap. He just sat there making stupid remarks. I looked at his head all over, not just the face, and I did all the sutures for him. Except his eye. That's why we kept him in—to wait till the swelling went down, so we could do it ... He must have been drinking ever since he went off at six, but how could I say so?'

I remembered the encounter when I'd gone to the autoclave room. 'He wasn't too clever before that, either.' I looked up at Randy. 'You didn't tell her any of that?'

'How could I? I wouldn't be believed. You know how the men stick together. One of the others would soon have said he was stone cold sober ... You and I are going to carry this, Clare, if the relatives do kick up.'

'Look, if they find the man who kicked him it could be a murder charge. And maybe it wasn't. Maybe it *was* the fall. But I'm sure in my own mind it wasn't.'

Randy showed the whites of his eyes. 'Oh, my God! I hadn't thought of that. But have they got him? Field went to his car to radio a description—that's why he wasn't there when the CO was playing up. But Emery didn't know his name.'

It was no use. Somebody had to do it. When Randy had gone off down the Casualty ramp I went back to Matron's office. Miss Corfield said: 'She's very busy, Nurse.'

'I know,' I said. 'I've just left her. But I must see her if she's alone. It's very important.'

'I'll just see if Mr. Sargent's gone, Nurse.' Was Matron discussing it all with him? I wondered. But there hadn't been time, because when Miss Corfield came back she said: 'Yes, all right, Nurse. Go in, will you?'

Matron looked up. 'Yes, Nurse? Something to add, I take it.' She seemed almost to have been expecting me.

'It isn't easy to say this, Matron. But I think someone must ... But it's very confidential. Mr. Fiske was supposed to have examined that man, Emery.'

'According to Mr. Brown he did, Nurse.'

'No. Matron, he'd been drinking that day. He wasn't fit: if he missed anything——'

'Nurse, you can't mean it?'

'I do. I can't prove it, but I know it's true.'

'Mr. Brown said nothing of this.'

'Matron, he wouldn't. He wouldn't expect to be believed, for one thing. For another, he's obviously not going to risk his job, is he? He has a wife and two little boys. He's far too much to lose.'

'And you haven't?'

'Not so much, no.'

'Nurse, I can't listen to you without some proof. You must know that.'

'If I got proof, would it help?'

She smiled. It seemed to me that she looked almost relieved. 'My dear good girl, of course it would. I know all about "the strongest trade union in the world" and so on. But the truth is the truth, and we have a strong profession too.'

'*Somebody* must know,' I said. Somewhere at the back of my head an idea was nagging to be recognised, but I couldn't identify it.

'Yes, Nurse. And if that somebody happens to be a doctor it may not help. You'll be on a sticky wicket, won't you?'

'I know, Matron. But don't you see, what I'm really trying to establish is that it's *not* Mr. Brown's fault, any of it. He's a good nurse. He's terribly conscientious. And he has a family to support. If somebody has to be sacrificed to pacify the relatives, or the Coroner, then it had better be me.'

She nodded. 'Your loyalty does you credit, Nurse ... Well, good luck with your detective work. That's all I can say, isn't it?'

It didn't occur to me then that she would discuss what I'd said with Neil Sargent. He—surely—was on the other side. 'Yes, thank you, Matron,' I said.

CHAPTER 5

A TEARFUL small boy and his mother met me on the ramp as I went on duty that night. She kept giving his upheld hand admonitory jerks as she lugged him along. 'Don't you never do that again!' she told him, talking at me. 'The nurses got plenty to do, wi'out you an' your barmy tricks.' Another jerk. I felt like telling her that we had enough to do, too, without dealing with dislocated shoulders.

Randy was drying his hands in the CO's room. 'What had *that* one pushed into his nose?' I asked.

He nodded at the receiver on the side table. 'Change from beads, anyway. Tofranil tablets, now! Mother's, of course.'

'Tofranil!' There were eight of the orange sugar-coated tablets in the dish. 'My God, he could have swallowed them! What would they have done to him?'

Randy shrugged. 'Convulsions, probably. And there's no real antidote—you can only treat the symptoms. Well, I told her about locking them up.'

'In at one ear and out at the other, I suppose. It often is,' I sympathised.

Randy grinned. 'Nothing in between to stop it, as Sister would say!' Then he sobered. 'Right, verbally as well as in the book, there are *no* in-patients. That child didn't see a doctor— Mr. Huxley's HS is supposed to be on call, but he's tied up in theatre. He says if you need anybody ring Toby Jarrett. And the CO takes over at ten. All right?' He glanced up at the clock. 'I'd better get my skates on.'

I didn't tell him about seeing Matron again. There was no time to begin that kind of conversation. 'Yes,' I said. 'Good-night, Randy.'

When he had gone I checked the book—the last item was signed: *R. Brown p.p. Cledwyn Jones*, which meant that he'd acted on instructions from a doctor accepting full responsibility—and then I did my round of the rooms. I got back to find an overalled workman waiting for me in the hall. He had a grimy bandage round one blue distended finger.

'Come along in,' I said. It was late to be still in his working clothes. 'Been working late?'

'No, Nurse. I got home at half five.' He looked down at his overalls. 'Felt too badly to change, tell you the truth. It's this finger.'

I threw the bandage into the bucket and looked at his hand. There was only a small lesion on the finger, but it was three times its normal size, and there was a great red ribbon of infection running up his forearm. 'It must have been giving you hell,' I said. 'Why on earth didn't you come before? How long has it been like this?'

'Coupla days. Chisel cut, see. I put some ointment on it, but it seems to a' gone bad ways. Give me gyp, it did, last night.'

Every time I heard the word 'ointment' I wanted to lose my temper. Ninety per cent of the people we saw in Casualty seemed to swear by some ointment as a cure-all. They smeared it on burns—making our work a lot harder—cuts, stings and every kind of skin lesion from chickenpox to warts. I controlled myself. '*Never* use ointment on dirty cuts,' I told him. 'Greasy things are just a breeding ground for germs. You need them to remove crusts, in things like impetigo—but then it's the grease, not the medication, that's useful. Otherwise you're safer to stick to watery solutions ... Undo your shirt, will you?' I felt under his arms. On the affected side his axillary glands were already knotted. 'Yes, I'm afraid you'll have to have it opened.'

He sighed noisily. 'Ar, that's what the missus said.'

'I'll get the doctor,' I said. 'When did you last eat?'

79

'Bit of a sandwich, midday. Cold boiled baby.'

'Cold *what*?'

'You never heard that? Cold boiled bacon, then. Haven't had nothing since. Didn't fancy it, some'ow.'

I didn't imagine that he would have done.

I got straight through to Toby Jarrett. 'Like to come and open a septic finger?' I said.

'For you, anything,' he told me gallantly. 'You're sure it needs opening?'

'Axillary glands plus plus. And only a tiny lesion that needs extending and draining. Pretty filthy.'

'I'll be there in two ticks.'

He was there by the time I had the trolley laid. 'He's not eaten,' I said. 'You can give him a whiff, if you want to.'

He leaned over the hand, wrinkling his nose. 'Well, we sure can't use a local on *that*. What about it, Mr.——?'

'Mr. Wilkins,' I supplied.

'Mr. Wilkins. It's going to hurt quite a bit—you'd like to go to sleep, wouldn't you?'

The man shook his head. 'No, I've got a horror of gas and that! You just get on an' do what you got to do, Doctor. I've had worse.'

'All right. Will you let me give you a little injection, then? You see it isn't the opening that'll hurt so much, it's the dressing afterwards.'

Mr. Wilkins was deeply suspicious of injections, too, it seemed. But eventually he agreed to 'the needle' as he called it, and I brought Toby the syringe and the Pentothal.

He was slow coming out of it, and I had plenty of time to put in a ribbon gauze drain and spin on tube-gauze from the thimble. 'Better lie down for half an hour,' I told him. 'Have a cup of tea before you go home, hm?'

'Gord, it don't half hurt!' he said.

'Yes. It'll be sore, I'm afraid. But Doctor will give you some sleeping tablets.' I looked up at Toby. 'Mogadon? We've got some in stock.'

'Yes, give him half a dozen to take home. And he's to come up tomorrow for dressing. All right?' He went over to the door.

'Stay right where you are,' I said. 'Somebody else coming up the ramp. Hold on while I put Mr. Wilkins on a bed.'

This time I put on cot sides automatically. Pentothal is odd stuff—its effects tend to return in waves. He was quite likely to fall back into a deep sleep again. Then I went back to Toby. He nodded at the grey-faced baby, grunting painfully in its mother's arms. She looked about sixteen, and probably was. No wedding ring, I noticed. 'Ring Kids',' he said. '*Stat.*' He bent to scribble out an admission slip.

'Pneumonia?'

'Uhuh.'

Children's said they would send a nurse down right away. 'Why do they always leave them till this hour?' Nurse Beckwith complained. 'I'll bet that kid's been ill all day. No sense, some of them. It makes me mad.'

'Me, too,' I said. 'But she's only a kid herself. Can she stay in?'

'I suppose so. She'll have to wait while I make the mothers' room bed up, though. Keep her with you for twenty minutes, will you?'

'Sure. But get the baby right away, won't you?'

'My girl's halfway there already.'

She must have been, too, because she came in at the ramp entrance with her ward blanket as I got back there myself, and carried the little creature up right away.

'Sure to be a third,' I told Toby. 'Just wait while I get these particulars, and then I'll make some tea. You'd like a cup, wouldn't you, Mother?'

Her name was Beatrice Kelly, and the baby's name was Gary, she told me. She lived in a bed-sitter five miles away. 'See, I work at Woolworth's,' she explained. 'The landlady, she keeps an eye on Gary for me. Got kids of her own, she has.'

Toby wasn't often bad-tempered, but he said sharply: 'It's to be hoped that she keeps a better eye on her own than she did on yours, then!'

I cut across him to explain to her about staying in. 'But I've got no night things with me,' she said.

'That's all right. They'll lend you a nightie and a dressing-gown. And a toothbrush.'

'But I can't stay away from work! I've got me rent to pay.' She looked scared stiff. 'Four pound ten, I have to pay for the room, and her minding Gary.'

'Disgraceful,' Toby said. He really wasn't helping, and I shot him the kind of look that ought to have told him so. Then I talked her down. Social security, our own Almoner and the rest. Then I made the tea.

I took the first cup through to Mr. Wilkins, and roused him to drink it. The second went to Beatrice Kelly. Toby and I took ours through into Sister's office. 'All right,' I said. 'Let off steam in here, not in front of the patients. What's biting you?'

He had calmed down now. 'Sorry. Oh, it just makes me mad, seeing kids get a raw deal. Not just the baby—the girl as well. Four pounds ten out of her wages for some sleazy little room and her baby "kept an eye on" by a slut who'd let it lie and die sooner than lift a finger!'

'Cool it,' I told him. 'Toby, you don't *know* that it's sleazy. Or that the landlady's a slut. And maybe that baby was pretty normal a few hours ago.'

'*Maybe*,' he said. 'Oh, well, let's talk about something else. What's the night-duty gossip these days?'

He was wide open asking for that. 'Oh, I hear rumours. About Leila Hamilton, for instance.'

He grinned. 'Just rumours? Not facts?'

'It's true, then?'

He stirred his tea contemplatively. 'I'm not going to be drawn on that one. It's all a deadly secret at the moment. So you can put that probe away, Clare. No comment.' He was still smiling.

'Fair enough,' I said. 'Just checking. I don't expect I'm alone. You know what the grapevine is—never idle.'

'Yes. Well, one thing I *can* confirm. If it says I'm taking Torfy Bates to the Faculty dance next Friday, then it's right.'

I frowned. 'Oh? Camouflage?'

'No. Pure pleasure. Actually what you might term a long-standing engagement. I always honour those. You know me.'

That was the trouble: I did, and it didn't help. 'I see.'

'Great girl, Torfy.'

'I know,' I told him. 'You're preaching to the converted. She has her mad moments, but she's a nice girl.'

He finished his tea, and looked at his watch. 'Right, ten o'clock. That lets me off the hook. From now on you can get the CO to do the dirty work for you.'

'Yes. *When* you've seen Mr. Wilkins off the premises. He ought to be fit by now.'

I didn't have to tell Toby that I had a temporary thing about having patients in the recovery ward at night. He and Mr. Wilkins walked down the ramp together. Then I directed the baby's mother to the ward, and she followed them. By the time she reached the low point of the ramp there was an ambulance in, and she had to stand aside as they brought the stretcher in. Two stretchers, in the end.

This time the motor-cyclist had got off lightly, but his pillion passenger, thrown over his head on to the tarmac, was out cold. He sat nursing his smashed hand, and saying: 'Her mother'll half kill her. And me.' I looked at the girl's stove-in forehead and the blood trickling from her left ear and reflected that there was nothing left for her mother to do, in that case.

I told the switchboard porter: 'I need the CO, straight away. Tell him there's a depressed frontal skull fracture, query fractured base as well, and a boy with a Colles' fracture and some fingers. And let Sister know, please.'

I got the particulars from the rider while we waited. The girl, he said, was only fourteen. 'She's not supposed to come on the bike,' he said. 'Been strictly forbidden, actually. Can *you* notify her people? I mean, her mother'll half kill me if I go round there, this time of night. They'll think she's in bed. They go themselves about half past nine, and she gets out through the window, you see. I mean, they're dead squares. Bed at half past nine, I ask you!'

I knew how Toby had felt, but I managed not to show it. 'And your name?' I said. 'Address? ... Age?' He was twenty-six. And if I was thinking that Betty was a bit young for him,

83

well, that was her fault. She was quick enough coming down to the club. Besides, the little dolly-birds were more fun than big ones.

Neil didn't have much patience with him, either. He ignored him until he had looked at the girl, and rung the SSO about taking her into Intensive. Then he took him into one of the cubicles in dressings to splint his hand pending X-ray and plaster in the morning. The young man was garrulous with shock-euphoria, by now, and began giving him the line about the little dolly-birds, too. Only now he went into all the details of exactly why they were more fun. Neil said: 'I don't need you, Nurse!' and waited for me to get clear of the section before he began talking himself. I didn't hear what he said, because I was handing over the girl to the orderly from Intensive, but in the background his voice rose and fell for several minutes.

He was thoroughly out of temper by the time the patient had gone, and he was washing his hands. When he took the towel from me I said: 'I don't know what's wrong with tonight. Every single person I've seen has been in a bad mood. Still, that boy made me see red, too.' I sighed. 'Now I'll have to ask Sister to send a police message. *He* wasn't going to tell the girl's parents. Why should he get off scot-free?'

'He isn't getting off scot-free, Nurse.' So I was back to 'Nurse' again. 'That hand won't be usable for at least two months, and maybe three. And he's a draughtsman.' That was more than I had found out. 'As to notifying the parents, you can do that yourself. They're on the phone. I'll speak to them too.'

His voice changed completely when he talked to the girl's mother. He was as gentle with her as he had been with Mrs. Rogers. As he had been with me, in his car, after the Rag dance. I asked myself what I had to do to earn his kindness again. Or was it his good opinion?

As he put the telephone down a patrol-car policeman put his head in. I knew him: his name was Andrews, and I had nursed him with gunshot wounds after he had tried to stop the getaway car from the Midland Bank robbery. I hadn't seen him for some time. He winked at me and then looked at Neil. 'Mr. Fiske?' he asked.

'Mr. Sargent is Casualty Officer now,' I said.

'Oh, sorry. I was told Mr. Fiske was. Just wanted to let him know about the case coming up.'

Someone came up the ramp and knocked at the door of the CO's room, so I left them at that point. It was only the Intensive orderly, come to return our blankets and plastic-covered pillow. The policeman had gone by the time I had put them away, and Neil was over by the office window, brooding out at the ambulance park. I poured myself another cup of tea from the cold pot I'd shared with Toby, and waited. This time he could begin the conversation: I didn't seem to be able to say the right thing.

After a while he said: 'The inquest on Emery's tomorrow. Half past ten. It'll be adjourned, pending enquiries and other proceedings. You won't be called.' He still didn't face me.

'I see,' I said. 'Is that what Andrews came about?'

'Oh? You even know their names? Your other friend was in earlier. Field, is it? Very popular with the force, aren't you?'

I didn't bother to explain about Andrews being an ex-patient, or about Peter Field. 'Am I?'

He swung round then. 'What else am I suppose to think? You were chattering to Field, making him tea, when that man fell out of bed, weren't you? And this man tonight comes in and—and winks at you.'

'He's been a *patient*,' I said, stung. 'And it may have escaped your notice, but patients *do* sometimes wink at nurses. It doesn't imply any lack of respect, either. Andrews had to converse that way when his jaw was wired after a g.s.w. He does it still, to show me he hasn't forgotten. Or wouldn't you understand that?'

'I don't understand anything about you. What *is* it with you, Clare? You've been having man trouble ever since I first met you. You were complaining then about Leckie. Then there was that business with Fiske. Then it's policemen. Don't you *know* when you're asking for trouble? ... And just what was Gibbon doing down here last night?'

He had a good memory. 'He came to get Parentrovite from the dispensary. Is that wrong?'

'Did he have to spend twenty minutes talking to you, as well?'

'I don't think he did.' And if he did, I thought, he's old enough to please himself. What the senior registrar does is hardly the CO's business.

'Look, I took Mrs. Rogers home. I saw her husband. We'd passed Gibbon on his way here. He was only just leaving when I got back. I suppose *he* had some tea with you, too?' He looked distastefully at the used cups on the tray. 'As Jarrett seems to have done tonight.'

'Yes, he has. And why not? It was a pot made originally for the Pentothal patient, and for a baby's mother, so why waste it? But since you're so interested, Jeremy Gibbon didn't have any on Sunday. My God, you sound like a spoiled, nasty, jealous little boy—or some kind of dictator! And all we discussed was Mr. Fiske's hangover, if you want to know.'

That was his chance to say something about Ken Fiske, about Emery's admission, but he didn't. It was the old story, I told myself. When doctors ganged up you couldn't win.

'I don't,' he said icily. 'And as far as I'm concerned you can entertain the entire house down here, and the police force *en masse*. Just so long as you don't neglect your patients while you indulge your—your hobby.'

'Neil! How could you!' But he wasn't listening. He was halfway down the hall.

I wanted to cry. It was so unfair. If I had been Sally Dane, I thought, or even Torfy, there might have been some justification for an attack like that. But to suggest that I, of all people, was what Sister Lamont would call 'man-mad' seemed utterly unjust.

No casualties arrived to distract me, and if they had I should have been dreading Neil's voice. The hard one he seemed to keep specially for me. I savagely tidied already tidy cupboards, telling myself how unfair he had been, until my relief arrived. I was surprised to find she was a new staff nurse, a set ahead of myself, a girl named Hodges. I said: 'Lordy, we *are* honoured. SRNs relieving now?'

'Sister Duffy thought you were a bit busy and might need me. The lights are still all on, and the CO must have been here for hours—you lucky creature.'

'My fault,' I said. 'I hadn't got round to turning out the hall lights. The CO's been gone for ages, and the flap's all over now, not that it was one... I'm not awfully hungry. What's for Meal?'

'Not bad at all. Mind, there are the usual harvest festival bowls of fruit, instead of a pud. But there's fresh salmon. The last feverish catch of the season, we gather. Toby Jarrett brought it in, and specified that it was for the night people.'

'Good for Toby,' I said.

'Plenty of gossip for you, too. At least, there was at first sitting.'

Meal on night-duty was the very root and stem of the grapevine. News always originated with the night people, and from them it filtered through to the day staff. Night nurses have more time to weigh up evidence, to collect facts from residents and to discuss them over tea-cups, and it is the same in any hospital. 'Such as?' I asked her.

'Well, uniform, for one thing. A lot of people have signed a protest, saying they don't want to wear paper caps, and can't we have the old ones back. Signed it myself, as a matter of fact. Well, they're just not professional-looking, are they? It's in the dining-room, if you want to sign. Minnie Cauthery's volunteered to take it to Matron ... And what else was there? Oh yes, police. Something about a chap named Emery. They wanted the path report or something, and they had to wait because Dr. Glaisher's on holiday, and the assistant did it. They're supposed to be charging some chap with murder?'

'Are you sure, Hodges?'

'Oh yes. Seems the man Emery was just walking along minding his own business and this great drunken Irishman decided to beat him up. Just come out of a pub, fighting drunk.'

It seemed to me that a lot of people had over-indulged on Saturday. It was only two, but it seemed a great many when they both connected with St. Finbar's. Those two had made a disastrous situation between them—and I was in the thick of it.

I wondered whether Neil knew that they had the man. He probably did. Perhaps that was what Andrews had told him. And he had been talking to Field earlier—he could have told him too. Then why hadn't he told me? Or were they planning to sit back and let the man stand trial without intervening? Ken Fiske might have been capable of doing that, but surely not the SSO. And surely not Neil Sargent. It was all wrong.

In the morning I checked with Horace to make sure. Before he became OP porter he had worked in a newsagent's shop right opposite the police station and the courts, and he had told me that he often got roped in as part of a coroner's jury. He would surely know the drill. I said: 'Horace, can anyone go to an inquest? Or is it only the people who are called?'

'Oh, they have to let the public in, Nurse. That's the law. Not that you often see many of the public there, mind you. Thinking of going to one, are you? Funny way to spend your off-duty. I know Nurse Bates likes to hear a good court case, but I think she draws the line at inquests.'

'And if it's going to be adjourned, what will they do?'

'Adjourned? Well, they'll just take evidence of death, and identification, and that. Then they'll close it. Not worth going to, is it?'

'No, perhaps not,' I said. 'Thank you, Horace.'

'My pleasure, Nurse.' I think that after working in OP for so long he was just about immune to silly questions. It was no sillier than those the patients would be asking him for the next ten hours or so.

'Small court,' the policeman in the foyer told me. 'Are you a witness, or public?'

'Public,' I said.

'This door, then. Plenty of seats in the dress circle, as you might say.'

He opened the door, and I slid into the first bench inside,

the back one of a steep bank of six. Humphrey Sumner, our SSO, was sitting down at the front—his cockscomb of red hair was recognisable anywhere, but there seemed to be nobody else from Fin's at all. There were one or two people on his bench, but nobody I knew. A reporter sat at a side table, and there were a few police milling about. They looked odd without their helmets, and a good deal younger, so that I didn't at first recognise Field. There was another one, standing against the wall, whose face I knew but whom I couldn't place, yet every time I looked at him some bell tried to ring at the back of my head. Something important, I was sure.

I had always thought that juries consisted of twelve people, but only seven elderly men filed into the jury box this time. The constable from the door had come inside now, and was standing at my elbow. He grinned at me and murmured: 'The seven dwarfs! They're all from the Sons of Rest, next door.'

When they had all been sworn—and it was rather involved because they all had to stand up so that they could reach the same bible—they creaked into their seats again, and the Coroner—whom I knew better as Dr. Williamson, once the assistant pathologist at St. Finbar's—murmured a little speech of which the only words I heard clearly were: 'James Emery, now lying dead.'

After Henry Maurice Emery, James's elderly brother, had given evidence of identification P.C. Field was called. He had been patrolling High Street on the night in question, he said, in his Panda car, and had been flagged down by a pedestrian who called his attention to a man lying on the bench by the horse-trough. The man—whom he identified as James Emery —was conscious, but appeared to have severe facial injuries. He had been attacked, he said, by a stranger who emerged from the Red Lion public house. 'I have his statement here, sir, if you wish it read,' he said. 'I took it from him at the hospital, and immediately contacted Information Room with a description of his assailant.'

Why, I wondered, did policemen keep a special vocabulary for court use? Field could never have *said*: 'Describe your assailant.' On the other hand, I supposed, he could scarcely stand up in court and say: 'A description of the chap who clobbered him.' And then I stopped wondering anything at all, because the faint bell at the back of my mind began to ring loudly as one of the policemen began to edge his way out, and another one joined it when it hit me that Field had said that the stranger had emerged from the Red Lion.

I managed to attract the door officer's attention again, and he bent his head to listen. 'That officer, just going out at the other door ... what's his name?'

He glanced across. 'That's P.C. Rawlings, miss. Teddy Rawlings, they call him. Why? You want a word with him?' His look said plainly enough: 'Fancy him, do you?' He was as bad as Neil Sargent. Why *did* people get the wrong idea of me?

'I merely want some information, that's all,' I told him coldly. 'Where can I find him?'

'You won't, now. He's gone back on patrol. Just been in for their canteen break, him and his mate. Popped in here to speak to the inspector, I think.'

I turned away from him and listened to what the Coroner was saying. '... adjourn these proceedings *sine die*. Will that suit you, Inspector?'

The inspector nodded, the reporter closed his notebook, everyone stood up, and once the Coroner had gone the jury scrambled out at the side door. 'Get their pocket-money now,' the doorman said, as I walked past him.

Humphrey Sumner caught me up on the steps outside. He looked surprised to see me. 'Hallo, Nurse! What have you been doing—parking in the wrong place?'

'Hardly,' I said. 'I've nothing to park.'

'In that case you'll need a lift. My car's just here.' He looked at me again. 'Or were you at the opening of that inquest?' Then it seemed to me that his jolly face clouded a little. 'Oh, of course. You're on Cas nights, aren't you?'

It was highly unlikely that the SSO would know what nurse worked where, unless he had special reason to. That meant that my name had been mentioned in connection with the Emery business. 'Yes,' I said. 'I thought I ought to hold a watching brief. I don't know what facts they propose to bring out, but they could be the wrong ones.'

'Well, if you have any information you shouldn't be holding it back. Have you?'

'I've one piece, yes. And I gave it to Matron. But she said I had to get proof. If I hadn't come here this morning I mightn't have got it, but now I think I have.'

He held open the door of his car for me. When he came round to the driving seat he said: 'Proof of what, Nurse Kennedy?'

'Sorry,' I said. 'It isn't anything you'll like, and I have to prove it first.'

'Well ... I'll like anything that will prove that we weren't negligent, and anything that will shed a little true light.'

I said: 'I'm awfully sorry, Mr. Sumner, but that may be a contradiction in terms.'

'I see.' He looked serious again. 'You'll be seeing Matron, will you?'

I nodded. 'As soon as I can make sense, yes.'

'Then we must leave it at that.'

He dropped me outside the Home, which was kind of him because it meant a detour. By that time I had remembered that Matron was off duty until Thursday.

That evening there was a BMA meeting of some kind in our nursing school lecture theatre. The residents' car park had overflowed into the ambulance park, and there was a packed mass of men in the front hall when we left the dining-room. We had to force our way through them, and Hodges said: 'Did you ever hear such a din? Talk about women clacking!'

'There ought to *be* some women,' I said. 'Where are all the female of the species?'

'Standing in for the men, of course. Isn't that typical? The women always are thin on the ground when they have these jamborees, and I'll swear it isn't because they're not keen ... Still, the main lecture isn't till half past nine, so maybe the women come late, like brides, after they've done the men's evening surgery for them.'

'Some brides,' I said. 'Leonora Kirk in bridal gear would make a splendid sight—rather like a whitewashed Statue of Liberty. I take it *you* won't be relieving me tonight?'

'No. My junior will—Hatherley. She's not a bad kid. A bit inclined to pursue the gentlemen in a kittenish sort of way, but on the ball nursingwise . . . Talking of the gentlemen——'

I stopped to rest my case on the radiator at the corner of the OP corridor. 'Yes?'

'I meant to tell you—when you were at Meal last night Jeremy Gibbon came down. He didn't want anything. He said: "What, no Kennedy?" and buzzed off again. Should I have offered coffee or something?'

'Shouldn't think so. He doesn't make a habit of calling on me, I can assure you. And if he'd wanted coffee he could have asked. Or made it himself.'

'He doesn't call? Oh. The grapevine had him down with you on Sunday night, too.'

I told her what I thought of the grapevine—it even had Neil Sargent in its toils, it seemed to me—and then I went on down to the department.

In the office I found Torfy pouring tea into one of Sister's best cups. 'Company?' I asked. 'The Minister dropped in, or something? We don't use those cups, *or* that tray-cloth, for anything less than the Chairman of the Regional Hospital Board, surely?'

'That's right,' she said. 'Take it through, and don't forget to curtsey. CO's room. Go *on*.'

I was mystified. 'Who, you idiot?'

'The chap who's lecturing this mob of quacks tonight. Tea he asked for, tea he gets. I never argue with high-ups.'

Still puzzled, I carried the tray through. There was a tall grey-haired man standing by the window. '*Father!*' I said. 'Why didn't you tell me?'

When he had hugged me he said: 'I didn't know, pet, until this afternoon. Bentley-Martin was supposed to be doing it, but he's had what amounts to pretty well a royal command, so I got hauled in instead. Thought I'd just say hello.'

'Lovely to see you,' I said. 'Here, tea. Torfy made it, I

didn't. Have it while it's hot, and I'll just see what's what. I won't be long.'

Torfy put her head through the door then. 'See? Told you it was a VIP.'

'Quite right,' I said. 'Torfy, any in-patients, anything pending, and so forth?'

'Not a thing. So I'm off. All right?'

'Right,' I said. 'Oh, with all this kerfuffle going on, and most of our people there, who's on call?' I remembered what Hodges had said. 'One of the women, I'll bet.'

'Wrong. Jeremy Gibbon of all people.'

'That'll make a change for him. We're not often honoured, are we?'

'How right you are! Well, goodnight. Goodnight, Professor. Nice to see you again.'

Father grinned at her. 'Mister will do, Torfy. You can leave the formalities to my students. Not that they *are* very formal these days.' When she had gone he looked me over. 'Bit pale, aren't you, pet? Not sleeping?'

'Not badly. It's the shock of seeing you here.' I hugged him again. 'How's Mother?''

'Oh, very fit.'

'What evening class is it *this* session? Mother's classes were a standing joke. 'She must have covered about everything by now, from leatherwork to pewter, and from Italian cookery to life-drawing.'

'Dear me, no, she hasn't. This time it's some kind of car maintenance for owner-drivers. Perhaps she'll now understand why she shouldn't pull out the choke button to hang her bag on. *That's* what I found her doing, last time she said her car "made a funny noise and wouldn't go properly"! She said: "Isn't that what it's for?".'

'Bless her,' I said. 'She'd never make a nurse. I don't know where she'd be with anaesthetic machines, and kidney machines and the rest of it.'

'Indeed,' he said. 'Clare, I really ought to go. Come and see us when you can ... Oh, and I was asked to bring you greetings from one of my young men. David Leckie. You remember him, do you? He said you would.'

'Yes,' I said, 'I remember him.'

Father's eyebrows twitched. 'Oh? You didn't like him very much?'

'Not very much,' I said. 'Conflicting chemistry.'

'He enquired most warmly.'

'Yes, I dare say he did ... Father, it's no joy being your child. All the ambitious young men look for consultants' daughters, and all the nice ones avoid them like the plague in case their motives are suspect. One of these days I shall change my name by deed poll ... No, I'm very proud of you, really, darling, but I don't like being chased by the David Leckies.'

He was amused. 'I fear I was one of them, once. And what did I get for marrying my chief's totally adorable daughter?'

'Me,' I said.

'Yes—and a woman who hangs her bag on the choke. Come to the door with me.'

I walked to the top of the ramp. 'Oh, talking of people who chase consultants' daughters—you know Dr. Hamilton, don't you?'

'Basil Hamilton? Yes, of course. Why?'

'There are rumours about his daughter getting tied up. The story runs that it's one of our men. Could you pump him?'

'Wretched child,' he said. 'Well, I'm not going out of my way, but if I see him I'll enquire. Will that do?'

'Yes, thank you. Everyone's dying to know.' That was an exaggeration—as far as I knew there were only two of us—but Father wasn't to know that.

The department seemed empty when he had gone. It would have been a relief to hear an ambulance pulling in. I took my time over the locking up, and then I opened the casualty book and turned back to the Sunday entries to copy an address on to the corner of my apron. Tomorrow I would call.

CHAPTER 6

It was soon after eleven that the ambulance men decanted a girl on to the couch in the CO's room. A plain-looking snub-nosed girl with knees too bony for her green mini-skirt and a Guide's tenderfoot badge on her hand-knitted white cardigan. She could have been any age from twelve to twenty, but between us we guessed fourteen. There didn't seem to be much wrong with her, except the fact that she was fast asleep. Her pulse was slow, but its volume was normal enough; she didn't smell of acetone, and she wasn't running a high temperature. They had brought her from the Hippodrome, they said, where a cleaner had found her sitting in the pit-stalls after everyone else had gone.

The driver said: 'Well, they've tried, we've tried, but it's no go. The cleaner had a go, and so did the manager.'

'Tried *what*?' I asked.

'To wake her up, Nurse. Now let's see what you can do.'

I knew more tricks than they did, but none of them worked. Even when I compressed her orbital nerve in the bony notch above her eye—which is painful enough to wake a sleeping elephant—all I got was a momentary flicker of her lashes. The same with the spots just in front of her ears: she even smiled faintly when I tried those—and then went on sleeping.

'Well, I'll have to get someone to see her,' I told them. 'We may have to wait, because our men are tied up at a meeting, so you may as well go.'

'Right,' the driver said. 'Here's her handbag, Nurse. The manager looked, but there's no name in it. Just a compact and a few tissues, and some jazz club tickets and about six bob in cash. The bobbies know about her, but they'll wait to hear from you if you want any help. OK?'

'OK,' I said.

I tried slapping her, and talking to her, when they'd gone;

and I checked her pulse again, and watched her respirations. They were simply slow, but that was all. Then I rang the switchboard. Maybe Jeremy would have ideas.

The porter said: 'You may have to wait a few minutes, Nurse. Is it very urgent?'

'Not particularly,' I told him. 'A few minutes aren't going to make any difference. A girl in some sort of a coma, but her condition's all right, as far as I can see.'

I should have learned not to express opinions like that. When I got back to her the girl had stopped breathing. It's a very odd thing how one notices that. A patient can breathe silently or noisily, easily or painfully, and a nurse registers the quality of it without much reaction. But when the breathing stops, that in itself is almost a positive sound. The silence is instantly noticeable. Especially in theatre, where even the spare nurse out in the scrub-room is alerted by it at once, and turns her head to see what is happening.

I was frantically trying to get a Brooke airway between her teeth when someone else's thumbs came down on either side of her jawbone, and the voice belonging to them said: 'Let me ... That's it. Right, you push and I'll blow.'

He went on inflating, and I went on pushing her ribs down, and between breaths he said: 'No piped oxygen?'

'Not down here,' I told him. 'There's a cylinder in Minor Ops, but no time to get it.'

That was when she began to breathe spontaneously. We watched her until we were sure, and then I had time to look at him. He was dark, with one of those moustaches that turn down at the ends. The kind that Ken Fiske had tried to grow, only this one was trimmed and tidy and matched the eyebrows above it. He was no bigger than Ken Fiske, either. In the relief of having the girl breathing again I said: 'Well! Enter a stranger in the nick of time ... I suppose you're a fugitive from the meeting?'

'Oh, it's over now, except for the gossip. The porter told one of your chaps that you wanted somebody, and he was a bit tied up, so I shot down out of curiosity.'

'Jolly good thing you did,' I said. 'Thanks.'

He slapped the girl's cheek lightly. 'Come on, girlie. Wake up.'

'And the best of British luck,' I said. 'Everyone else has tried.'

He looked up sharply. 'How d'you mean?'

'That's why she's here.' I explained how we had come by her, and listed the ways I'd tried to wake her.

'I *wonder*,' he said. 'Got an evening paper?'

I nodded. 'Sister usually leaves hers for the night nurse. Hold on, and I'll look.' It didn't even strike me as an odd request. I was just naturally playing nurse to his doctor. At least, I assumed he was a doctor. He would hardly have been at the meeting if he wasn't. And he seemed to know what he was doing.

The paper was on the table in the office, where she usually left it, and I took it back to him. 'Right,' he said. 'Let's see what *was* on at the Hippodrome.' He turned to the entertainments column on page two and folded it back. Then he smiled. There was something familiar about that smile—it reminded me of someone else—but I couldn't pin it down, and I didn't try just then. 'Yes,' he said. 'That was inspired guesswork, if you like!' He looked up at me. 'Well? Diagnosed it?' He looked remarkably pleased with himself.

I shook my head. 'Not unless ... Well, we had a girl in a few weeks ago, from the discothèque. The SMO said it was an induced epilepsy. Something to do with all those psychedelic lighting effects. I suppose it was a kind of stroboscopic thing.'

He showed very white teeth. 'Try again.'

'I've no idea.'

He put the paper on the foot of the couch and tapped the place with the back of his fingers. 'Read it.'

Of course I was furious with myself for not thinking of it too. Torfy would have done, I was sure. There it was, the main attraction of the week. *MORPHOS—The Showbiz Hypnotist*. 'Clever stuff,' I said. 'Why didn't *I* think of that? Dim, that's me.'

'She must have accepted some sleep-suggestion meant for victims on the stage, and didn't hear the waking instructions, I suppose.'

'Fantastic,' I said. 'Oh well, we must wait and see what First On decides to do about it. There must be somebody who can wake her. It's a pity Colonel Findlay-Smith isn't here.' The name obviously didn't mean much to him. 'Our dental man,' I explained. 'He's done extractions under hypnosis, according to the SEN in Minor Ops.'

'Ah yes. He was the chap who did it on television, wasn't he? White hair, black eyebrows?'

'That's the one.'

'If you've a phone handy, I think we ought to try to find out where this Morphos chap's putting up for the night. I could do that for you. You're probably going to need him, you know.'

'Would you? There's a phone in Sister's office—the last room on the right.' It seemed to be the only constructive thing to do.

I was in the middle of explaining to Jeremy Gibbon when he came back. 'Rang the theatre,' he said. 'Only cleaners there, but at least they were able to give me the manager's home number. Rang that, he wasn't home yet. But his wife says Morphos is putting up at the Albany.' He showed his teeth again. 'Under the name of Jack Outhwaite. Not very romantic.' He looked at Jeremy with the kind of friendly respect a very junior houseman has for his chief. 'So if you do need to ring him, sir ... It's Midland eight-one-seven-one. And now I'd better be off.'

Jeremy blinked at him. 'Oh. Well, thanks very much, old man. Very good of you.'

'Not at all. Sheer nosiness on my part ... Goodnight, Nurse.'

'Goodnight,' I said. 'And thanks for the help with the airway. She's got such a silly little mouth, that——'

He laughed at that, as I walked to the door with him. 'And you'd got such a silly big airway!'

'The first one I saw in the cupboard.' The near-familiarity of that laugh made me say it: 'I'm *sure* we've met before.'

He nodded. 'Yes. But I didn't labour the point. You obviously didn't recognise me, and it must be nearly ten years ago.

I was a pretty nasty little specimen in those days. Still, I hope you've forgiven me by now.'

I was still staring after him when Jeremy said, in his pained-patience voice: 'If you've quite finished reminiscing ...'

Somehow I snapped out of it, shelved it until there was time for personal considerations. Right now there wasn't. 'What I can't understand is why she should stop breathing. We had to resuscitate her. If there's nothing wrong with her ...'

'Probably because all her reactions were so slowed up that she'd come to the point of no return breathingwise, for the moment. She'd probably have begun again spontaneously without any resuscitation, if you'd given her time. There'd have been a big enough build-up of carbon dioxide to make her. It isn't exactly easy for normally healthy people to die, you know. Nature fights against it tooth and claw ... Right, well, fetch a trolley then.'

'Trolley?' I looked at him blankly. '*Trolley?*'

He sighed. 'Theatre trolley, ducky. Or a wheelchair. To take her to the phone. Got it?'

It was all so simple. Jeremy got Jack Outhwaite on the line and did the explaining; we put the receiver to the girl's ear; we heard his voice, and three finger-snaps, and that was it. She sat up, smiled at us vaguely and said: 'What have I done with my handbag?' She didn't seem in the least surprised to find herself at Fin's. Jeremy said afterwards that Morphos—or rather Jack Outhwaite—had said he would give her the right suggestions before he woke her, so that she wouldn't be startled. It was all a great big mystery to me.

At least I had been right about her age. Her name was Beryl Adams, and she lived three streets away, and she thought she'd better go now, because her mum might be wondering where she was. That was that. Then, pouring out coffee for Jeremy and myself, I thought aloud: 'I can't believe it!'

Anyone else would have thought I was talking about the girl, but Jeremy didn't. 'Voice from the past? And was *he* one of the ungentlemanly ones? Am I right?'

'You're always right.' For no sensible reason at all I began to cry. 'I'm the one who's always wrong, remember. That proves it, doesn't it?'

'*That's* not very sensible, is it? Here you are, lovely big hanky, specially kept for weepy nurses ... How much sugar do you have?'

'I don't ... It was a sh-shock.'

'Yes. So you'll have two. Put your blood-sugar up.' He stirred my coffee and pushed me down into Sister's chair. 'Come on. Drinkies.'

He was very sweet, and if Neil Sargent had walked in and caught him I don't think I should have cared at all. Jeremy would have been quite capable of explaining everything, with no effort from me at all. I said: 'You're very nice sometimes, Jeremy.'

'Only sometimes? Oh dear. That isn't what my other lady-friends tell me.'

'Always, then. Especially tonight, I mean. Things have got on top of me a bit, and that was the final straw.'

'Seeing him, or finding out how wrong you'd been?'

I stopped mopping my eyes to look at him. 'How did you know that?'

'Because I'm a witch. Didn't you know? ... I see it all in the crystal. You had a thing about him, you've let it build up for years, and now you've shed it in the cold light of reality. Right?'

'Something like that,' I admitted.

'Yes. The trouble with you is that you haven't learned to shrug things off. The past's the past. It's dead. Tomorrow isn't here yet. So—live for today. You can't *alter* yesterday, ducky. But you *can* alter your attitude to it. Turn some of the bogeymen into normal human beings, hm?'

I blew my nose, and drank some coffee while I thought about that. 'He—he was rather nice, wasn't he? And he did know what he was doing.'

'Yes. And how had you been seeing him?'

I told him all about Ted Gaunt then, just as I'd told Neil on the night of the Rag ball. 'It was so silly of me to be surprised that he was a doctor, because the reason we *went* to this stupid dancing class together was because my father and Dr. Gaunt were friendly—they used to stand in for one another some-times—and so our mothers used to get together and talk kids together.'

'And you didn't know he was a quack? How very odd.'

'It's not. They moved away, London or somewhere, and we didn't see them any more.'

'No, but—— Did your papa come to see you tonight? You knew he was here?'

'Oh yes. He came down before the lecture.'

'I see.' Jeremy looked mysterious. 'So if he didn't tell you, perhaps he'd been asked not to?'

'Tell me *what*?'

'Well, *I* had Gaunt introduced to me by your aged p. As his houseman.'

'Oh no! Of course, David Leckie will have moved on up by now ... But why didn't he *tell* me?' Then I realised. 'Oh, I know why he didn't. I made quite a speech about housemen who chase consultants' daughters. Reference David Leckie, actually, but Father probably thought it wouldn't be politic to mention Ted Gaunt after that.'

'Probably. Knowing your speeches. You don't mince words when you really get on your little soapbox.' Jeremy smiled. 'I expect it's something you catch from Torfy. She doesn't pull her punches, either.'

'Not always,' I said. 'She can be as secretive as the devil when she likes.'

'Clare, what do you *do* in your off-duty?'

'Nothing very inspiring. Laze. Read. Go shopping when I have to. Coffee with the girls sometimes. Why?'

'Don't you go out with old Torfy?'

'Joke over,' I said. 'She's always out with someone else. You ought to know that—it was you until recently.'

'Ah, but who is it now?'

I thought about Toby and the Faculty dance, but if Toby was tied up with Leila Hamilton maybe it wouldn't do to mention that. 'She's in a transition phase, I think.'

'Anyhow, it isn't me. So I'm as free as the air, at the moment. Isn't it lovely? I can go out with someone else without the grapevine saying I'm two-timing. You, for example.'

'*Me?*'

'Why not? It would be a new experience.'

'Oh, Jeremy, there are dozens of girls at Fin's who'd love to be taken out. Don't waste your time on *me*.' He never had, in more than three years. I didn't see why he should begin now, except that I knew he was trying to be kind.

'Rubbish. You go back to days on Saturday?'

'In theory. Actually I get days off then.'

'Right. I'll pick you up from the Home, around seven-thirty on Saturday. That's if you still want me to. If not, we'll scrub it.'

'Are you serious?' I said. 'I never can tell with you.'

'I know. It's part of my repulsive charm. Goodnight, ducky, and don't cry any more. Bad for the face. And it's not at all a bad face, as faces go.' He smiled. 'If I wasn't afraid you'd get swelled head I'd tell you that you're the easiest thing to look at in Cas at the moment.'

'Well, there are only two of us here!'

'I *meant* among the full Cas staff. But let it pass.' He put the cups in the sink before he went.

When Nurse Hatherley came down to relieve me she said: 'The food's fantastic. Great trays of stuff left from the BMA do. Canapés and things we're supposed to take back to the wards to eat with our four o'clock cuppa. What's all this about a girl being hypnotised, Nurse?'

'Mr. Gibbon does get around, doesn't he?'

'Well, yes. He usually comes up to us for some tea about midnight. I think he's sweet on old Hodges, actually.'

That explained a lot of things: Hodges' probing, her possibly edited account of his visit on Monday when I was at Meal. '*Is* he, now?' I said.

'Not that he ever asks her out, or anything. Still, there's always hope, I suppose. But he's a bit old for her, isn't he?'

'Old?' I said. '*Old?* He's forty-one, that's all.'

'Is he that much? Well, there you are. That's what I mean.'

Hatherley was about nineteen, maybe twenty. I wondered what happened to girls of twenty, who thought forty-one old, so that at twenty-one it seemed fairly contemporary. 'Rubbish, Nurse,' I told her. 'Mr. Gibbon's just in his prime!'

'That's exactly what Hodges says ... Makes him sound like Miss Jean Brodie, doesn't it?'

'Wait a year, Nurse. In a year's time you may see him through different eyes.'

I don't know what she made of that. Certainly I didn't much care. She would probably repeat it all to Hodges, and I didn't care about that either. It seemed to me that he was the only person who had been kind to me for a long time. That wasn't true, of course; it was just the effect he'd had on me. He was kind, and he didn't even expect to hold my hand, and that was very comfortable.

Torfy was off on Wednesday. She was waiting in my room in her dressing-gown, when I climbed up there after dinner.

'You're not going to bed,' she announced. 'You're coming out, and I don't mean maybe. Lovely weather like this ... You're wasting it.'

I had my own plans. 'I'm too tired to rush about. You know what you are—you're like an unbroken pony let loose.'

'All right. If you want to sit down we could go to court. But it's only motoring offences on Wednesdays. You can go to sleep there though, if you like. In the public library they come and poke you awake.'

I sat down and kicked off my shoes. 'Do they? Why?'

'Heaven knows. To discourage the spivs, I suppose. Do you know where the word "spiv" comes from? "Suspected Persons, Indigents and Vagrants." It's a police classification I suppose. Well, it was a policeman who told me. Anyhow, they want to discourage them from going in the library for a kip, I imagine. They don't go, once they get the message that some bony-fingered librarian's liable to dig them in the ribs every quarter of an hour.'

I said: 'Talking of policemen, do you know a patrol-car driver called Rawlings?'

'Don't think so. Should I?'

'He was here on Sunday, with that Imp crash.'

103

She frowned. 'And?'

'Look, do you want to help Randy Brown? And me?'

'Sure, but——'

'Rawlings knows that Ken Fiske was pickled on Saturday. And *he* isn't a doctor, so he won't mind repeating it.'

'To whom?'

'Well, Matron said I had to be able to prove it, and——'

'Dear girl, you surely don't imagine any policeman's coming here to talk to Matron for you, do you? It's asking a bit much. They could probably be in trouble if they did things like that.'

'They're supposed to be public servants,' I said obstinately. 'He *knows*, because he told me so. And it must have been *before* he came in to examine—or rather non-examine— Emery. Randy won't say so, because he's afraid of not being believed. But if a *policeman* said so he would.'

Torfy shook her head over me in that pitying way she had. 'Listen, stupid. If Ken Fiske was out in his car, drunk, and they didn't stop him, they can't now afford to mention it, can they? And if they *did* stop him, then it's *sub judice* and they still can't discuss it.'

'Maybe they did,' I said. 'Andrews came looking for him and said something about a case coming up, only I didn't think of that at the time.'

'Winky Andrews?'

'Yes. I thought it was one of the inquests he'd come about, though.'

'Well, think about coming out, while I have my brek.'

I looked at my watch. 'It won't be over for another hour, yet.'

'Want to bet? Why do you think William doesn't do any OP jobs till after nine-thirty?'

'No. Tell me.'

'Because till then he's kitchen porter. So he's putting my tray in the laundry-lift at eight-forty precisely.'

'And I was wondering what William had that Horace hadn't. So that's it.'

'Not that Horace isn't a little gem.' She stood up and

stretched her arms above her head. She could nearly touch the lampshade. Her flame silk kimono sleeves fell back from her knobbly wrists.

I said: 'Torfy, you're frightfully thin.'

'My dear, I eat and eat, and it makes no difference at all. When I was small my brothers called me "Skinny Liz from the boneyard", and they still do. Not to worry.'

'I shudder to think what your metabolic rate can be.'

'So? I'm not exophthalmic, am I?'

'Take your glasses off.' I looked hard at her eyes. 'No. But isn't it Hashimoto's disease that isn't? Anyway, I'm watching you.'

Via exophthalmia, *via* the hypnotic eye, I got round to telling her about Beryl Adams and Morphos. I didn't mention Ted Gaunt—I wasn't used to that myself yet—but I did mention Jeremy. 'You know what?' Torfy said. 'It'd do you good to run around with old Jeremy for a bit. You couldn't possibly feel safer with anyone, and he's very understanding.'

It was nice to be able to surprise her. 'That's just what I'm proposing to do, as a matter of fact. On Saturday.'

'You *are*?' She stared at me. 'Well, jolly good for you. What brought that on, apart from all the psychological delving you seem to do at L-J's clinic?'

'Nothing. He just asked me. I suppose he misses *you*, you idiot. Doesn't that occur to you? It's the same as a girl cultivating a man's best friend to get a line on him.'

'Quite. What do you imagine I was doing when I cultivated Jeremy? If he isn't Toby Jarrett's buddy, then who is?'

I began to wonder just how devious Torfy could be. But at least it released me to be a little underhanded myself. While she was eating her breakfast I changed, checked the address on my apron corner, and left the Home without telling her.

The curtains were all closed, and that was Albert Street language for 'we haven't yet had the funeral'. It seemed to me that a call simply wasn't on, in the circumstances. But as I turned to walk away Mrs. Rogers came running down the little path to the gate. 'Nurse!' she said. 'Nurse, it *is* you, isn't it?

Yes, I thought I recognised you. Won't you come inside for a minute?'

It is one of those strange facts of life that whereas nurses are notoriously unable to recognise patients once they have discarded their pyjamas and put on clothes, patients and their relatives invariably recognise a nurse they have seen only in uniform, even if she wears a wig, loads her face with make-up, and puts on skirts twelve inches shorter. And I wasn't wearing a wig, or very much make-up, and my duster coat was two years old and hardly mini. I said: 'Yes, from Casualty. I wondered whether you'd remember me.'

'Of course I do. You were so kind on Sunday night. You and the doctors.' I was glad she made it plural, after saying that Janey wasn't a 'proper' doctor. 'Come in, dear. Sit down.' She bustled me into the correct little parlour, with its regulation three-piece suite, standard lamp, china cabinet and TV set. One of those rooms that are used only on Occasions. This was an Occasion, obviously. 'The funeral's tomorrow,' she told me. 'You see, they only had the inquest yesterday afternoon. There were five yesterday altogether, the policeman said. Will you come, dear? Twelve o'clock from the house.'

I said that since I was on nights I had to be in bed by twelve, and apologised. 'Otherwise I'd have come,' I said. It was amazing how much she had perked up since Sunday night, but I'd seen it happen before. Those who were most grief-stricken at the time seemed to get their tears over and gather new strength to do all the practical things quite quickly; those who controlled themselves often grieved for long months afterwards. We'd been told about that, in our lectures on the psychology of the nurse–patient relationship: we knew that people should be encouraged to express their grief, and not stifle it. Just as we knew that small children who had traumatic experiences should be urged to talk about them, and go on talking about them until they were sick of the subject; because if they were told to 'forget it' that was precisely what they didn't do. I knew that now from personal experience: I knew that if I had talked to my mother about Ted Gaunt, been made to repeat it to my father, and to go over it again and

106

again until I grew bored, I should never have let the incident become the burrowing, growing, mental tapeworm it had been for ten years, that had coloured my whole outlook. So I was glad that Mrs. Rogers had let go on Sunday, once and for all, and was now climbing towards being herself again. I said: 'Yes. The first inquest was on a man who was beaten up on Saturday, but they've adjourned it.'

'Oh yes. A terrible thing, that!'

'Mrs. Rogers, you did say your husband went to the Red Lion sometimes. Do you think— Well, was he there last Saturday? Would he know anything about it?'

'Well, yes, he saw it. It was him stopped the Panda car, and told them.' She leaned forward. 'Why, dear? You look worried.'

I said yes, I was, and I explained pretty roughly why, without naming any names, least of all my own. 'Do you remember exactly *what* your husband saw?'

'He saw this big fellow come out of the Lion—he was just on his way in, see—and start beating up this Mr. Emery for no reason. Just walking along, he was. Knocked him down, and kicked him.'

I leaned forward. '*Where* did he kick him?'

'Where, dear? Why, his head, I thought he said.'

'Anywhere else?'

'I don't remember, to tell you the truth. You'd have to ask Ron when he comes home from work.'

I got out a pen and tore a page from my diary. 'Look, Mrs. Rogers, do you think he'd telephone me this evening? This is the hospital number, and he must ask for Nurse Kennedy in Casualty. It really is very important.'

'I'm sure he will, dear. He's got to go to the police station tonight, to make a statement, so he can do that on the way. See, they didn't bother him till now, on account of our bit of trouble. They said if he went in tonight it'd be all right.'

'I see. Yes, ask him to ring me *before* he goes to the station, if he can. But I don't go on duty till nine, so——'

'That'll be all right, Nurse. He won't be home till after eight himself. Working overtime, dear, to make out for a day off tomorrow . . . Now, can't I make you a nice cup of tea?'

I explained that I was supposed to meet Torfy, and asked her to excuse me. It would have been nice to be able to give her the money for the phone call, but I knew it would have hurt her feelings. At least I wasn't going to drink her tea, so maybe that made it even.

Torfy came into the Singing Kettle just before eleven, as I'd thought she might. We had a standing arrangement to meet there, on the hour, if we missed one another. 'You outsize rat,' she said. 'Where've you been? Is that my coffee? Thanks.'

'I've only walked down to Albert Street and back. You wanted me to get out, didn't you?'

'What on earth is there in Albert Street, apart from rows of houses, all with plaster Alsatians in the windows?'

'Not all,' I told her. 'I spotted one with Boy with a Thorn in his Foot, and one with yellow chrysanthemums in a cut glass vase. Where have *you* been?'

'Chasing up your P.C. Rawlings. He's due in court with a traffic case at half past twelve, they reckon. So we'll go back.'

'We?' I said. 'I'm not. I'm going to bed.'

In the end we compromised. I agreed to walk as far as the court with her, and to look in the foyer for Rawlings. After that she would stay and I would go back to hospital.

Rawlings wasn't anywhere to be seen. But if he had been I doubt whether I would have spoken to him, because Neil Sargent was coming out of the door marked *Coroner's Officer*, and looking straight at us.

I don't know what happened to Torfy: she simply ceased to be at my side. That left me face to face with him, and his face was giving nothing away. It didn't even tell me whether or not we were on speaking terms again. His grey eyes studied me thoughtfully and he didn't smile. But at least he didn't turn away. Neither did I, because my legs were suddenly trembling so much that if I had tried to negotiate the steep front steps of the court I should very likely have fallen headlong down them to the pavement.

Something like about two months later he said: 'I asked Torfy to bring you. Will you drive back with me?'

I didn't have any real choice, because he took a firm grip on my elbow and led me down the steps and through the gate into the police car park. 'I want to talk to you,' he said, in the car. 'Where shall we go? Would you like some coffee?'

I'd had two cups already, but I nodded. Something had happened to my throat and I knew my voice wouldn't come out the right shape.

'Good,' he said. 'Is that Cherry Tree place all right?'

I nodded again. It would be full of loud-voiced women with Minis lined up outside full of shopping, but nobody from St. Finbar's ever went there, and that was what mattered.

He found a table in a corner, half hidden by a Japanese screen. The women at the other tables sounded like mad hens, but we were in a still centre of our own. After they had brought our coffee, and he had poured both cups, and sugared his own, and stirred it for a long time he said: 'I think I owe you an apology, first of all, Clare.'

I lifted my head quickly. 'For what?' It came out as a husky croak, so I tried again. 'For what, Neil?'

'Several things. But principally for the things I said on Monday night. I'd had one or two shocks, but it was still inexcusable of me. You see, I was worried about the man Emery. It had begun to look as if—well, as if you might have to carry the can over that. I was angry *for* you—and I projected it into anger *with* you. Do you understand?'

I knew all about projection. About mothers, frantic to find missing children, who smacked them when they found them. About the way I'd projected my own childish fear of Ted Gaunt—which I saw now for what it was—on to David Leckie, and Ken Fiske, and a whole lot of other people. 'Yes, I think so,' I said.

'And then Brown came and talked to me this morning.'

'Staff Nurse Brown? Randall?'

'The Jamaican lad, yes ... He told me, quite categorically, that he didn't inform you that Emery was in, and that he blamed himself bitterly for not putting up cot sides. Clare, *why* did you try to cover up for him?'

I drank some coffee before I answered. It was very hot and

strong, and it made my eyes run. 'Look,' I said at last. 'He's got a wife, and two kiddies. He can't afford trouble.'

'And you can? I hear you told Miss Macintosh that you were ready to take the blame. To be "sacrificed to satisfy the relatives", or some such phrase. Did you?'

'She had no right to tell you that. Randy mustn't lose his job,' I said stubbornly. 'You're not to involve him, no matter what he told you.'

'He told me something else, too. And *that* was risking his job, or would have been if I'd been some COs I can think of.'

I waited, saying nothing.

'He says that Fiske didn't examine that man at all. And that *he* looked only at his face and head.'

'That's probably absolutely true,' I said. 'Randy's a very honest person.'

'He says that Fiske was drunk. But that he didn't say so before because he didn't think he'd be believed.'

'I know. So why has he come forward and said it now?'

'It appears that he talked it over with his wife, and he decided to come to me and tell me everything, purely and simply because they didn't want to see *you* blamed for what happened.' He smiled very faintly for the first time. 'You're all being so beautifully loyal to one another that it confuses the issue rather.'

Tina was a nice girl: it must have cost her a lot to encourage Randy to speak up. 'Isn't that what doctors do too?' I said. 'The strongest trade union, etcetera?'

'Is that what you think? That I'd cover up if I honestly thought Fiske was to blame?'

'And wouldn't you? You'd be odd man out if you didn't.'

He shook his head. 'You don't know me very well, Clare. I'm concerned with the truth, that's all. But to agree that Fiske was negligent isn't the same as saying he was responsible for the man's death, is it?'

I pushed my cup forward and he refilled it. 'Thank you. Neil, if he'd been thoroughly examined earlier, and you'd known all there was to know, and he'd been admitted to a ward, could he have been saved?'

'The pathologist says it's doubtful.'

'Then this man they're holding—this Irishman——'

'His name's Flaherty.'

'Then Flaherty *will* be charged with murder?'

'We shall know that tomorrow ... Clare, let's not go on talking about Emery for the moment—that's incidental to the fact that I wanted to apologise to you.' He put more sugar in his cup and stirred it again, watching the swirls from the spoon as intently as if they had been pyloric waves on a baby's stomach. 'Perhaps we could somehow begin again where we left off last year? Could we? Things seem to have got out of hand, and out of proportion.'

'Yes,' I said, 'they have.' It all began to well up again when I thought of it, and I had to say it. 'How *could* you suggest that I'd precipitated a "squalid little scene" with Ken Fiske? And make all that stupid fuss about poor Winky Andrews?' I began to upset myself all over again. 'And look how you went on about Jeremy Gibbon. It wasn't even your affair what he did.'

'A squalid little scene? *Did* I blame you for it?'

'Oh yes. You said: "That was a squalid little scene, wasn't it?" Surely you remember.'

'Yes, I remember saying it—but not as a criticism of *you*. I meant that Fiske had behaved badly, and I was sorry you'd been exposed to it ... Oh dear! To be honest I was so furious on your behalf that I don't know quite how I did put it. All I wanted to do was to thump the little beggar hard. If I'd got rid of my aggression that way it might have been better than doing it verbally, mightn't it?'

'That's what Flaherty did, though,' I pointed out. 'The other day there was some programme on TV—I read about it in the evening paper—when somebody said that we needed war. That the reason for hippies, and hooligans, and vandals, and drug addicts, and all the other anti-social things, is that we need a war for people to work off their violence in. And he said all schools ought to play rugger, because it's violent, and that soccer's too clean to give them a chance to be violent ... Why

111

are we all so full of violence, Neil?'

'We? Are you, Clare?'

'Oh yes. But it never gets out. I suppose I translate it into energy or something, work it off ... Torfy must have an awful lot of it in her, the amount of energy she develops.'

'Perhaps it's all a question of adrenalin, after all? If we all had adrenalectomy, by law, as babies, mightn't it be a more peaceful world?'

'No. Because we'd all have low blood pressure and be dull and lazy and miserable. And we'd have too much pituitrin and——'

'We'll continue that discussion later. Clare, I have to go now. Miss Watts has anaesthetics to do at twelve-fifteen. And you're ready for bed ... *Are* we on terms again?' He held out his hand.

I gave him mine. His palm was warm and dry and mine was tingling with static. It was a very odd sensation, and it spread up my arm so that I let his go again quickly. 'Yes,' I said. 'Drop me where you dropped me after the Rag ball, and let's try again.'

In the car I said: 'You know, Ken Fiske *was* drunk, as Randy says. And I can prove it. There's a policeman who'll confirm it, as a matter of fact. So you mustn't think Randy's lying.'

'I don't Clare ... There's something I ought to tell you. I didn't know until Monday, myself, and it's the reason why I'm glad I *didn't* go for him physically. I wouldn't have forgiven myself if I had. And I don't think I'll forgive you if you do produce this policeman as proof.'

'Oh? What, Neil?'

'Understand, I don't think anyone knows except Dr. Glaisher, at present. Maybe the SMO. And *this* is why they'll all gang up to save Fiske—*not* through any professional *esprit de corps*.' He turned to glance at me. 'Clare, Ken Fiske was diagnosed last Thursday as an acute leukaemia. He's a very frightened little man.'

'*No!*'

'Do you know where he's gone?'

112

'London, we heard. Another job, we assumed.'

'Not a job, no. He's gone into hospital as a patient. Glaisher's a close friend of Hartley Shapperley's, and if he can't help neither can anyone else.'

'Well, Shapperley's done a lot of research, hasn't he? Folic acid antagonists and all that.' And research, I reflected, was about all it had amounted to, so far. People had remissions but they weren't cured. Maybe the remissions lasted a little longer, and that was the most that could be said. 'One more guinea-pig,' I said.

'Don't be defeatist, Clare. They *could*—any day—come up with something.'

'And he was told on Thursday?'

'Last Thursday morning. He went over to the path. lab after breakfast to see Glaisher.'

Thursday, I thought. The day Horace had said that the CO was 'not in a very happy mood', that he was behind with his work and had tangled with Sister Lamont. The day he had been so difficult as I trundled the drum-trolley up the ramp ... 'I feel a complete heel,' I told Neil.

'I think that's when the drinking began, Clare.'

I nodded. 'Yes. Let's be fair—I've never known him do it before. Never. Oh, *why* didn't he tell somebody?'

'Would you? If nobody liked you very much?'

'Is this your real reason for wanting to talk to me? Because you knew I was gunning for him?'

'No. The most important thing was to make friends with you again. Then I knew I had to tell you.'

'Is it a secret?'

He paused to consider. 'No. Not a secret. A private personal matter. If you can draw the distinction. Is there someone you want to tell?'

'Yes. I need to tell Randy and Torfy—but there's someone else as well. At least, I don't know how deep it went——'

'A girl? Because if there *is* a girl who's affectionate towards him, perhaps she should go to him.'

'Yes. I think I'd have to see what Torfy thought.'

We were not far from Fin's now. I wondered if he would

remember where he had dropped me last time. He said: 'You're very fond of Torfy, aren't you?'

Was I? Sometimes Torfy and I were miles apart. 'Well, I admire her. She does all the things I'd like to be able to do. Mixing with people. Trying anything once. I'm no good at it. I don't have her confidence. She's fun, sometimes, and she makes me feel dull.'

'You? Dull? No, Clare, don't see yourself like that. Quiet, perhaps. A little shy. Not *dull*. Obstinate, of course!'

He was smiling as he pulled up just beyond the OP gate, in the exact spot where he had left me after the Rag ball. 'I think this is where we came in,' he said.

'Yes. Goodnight, Neil.'

His eyebrows went up. 'A night nurse's goodnight, or a Rag goodnight?' Then he leaned over, as he had done then, to open the door for me. I saw, as I had seen then, how his thick, springing hair grew to a point at the back of the neck. I still hadn't asked Torfy what it said about that in her phrenology book. 'Goodnight, Clare,' he said. Only this time he put one hand over mine as he said it. The tingle persisted all the way to the Home.

CHAPTER 7

TORFY was back already, lying on her bed with her shoes off and the door open, reading *The Heart People*. She said. 'Oh, so there you are. Look, I couldn't get hold of Rawlings, but I did have a word with Andrews, and——'

'Never mind that,' I said. 'So all your eagerness to make me walk up to court with you was just directed by Neil Sargent, was it?'

'That's right.' She gave me a defiant little look. 'Hell, I

114

knew him long before you did. Why shouldn't I oblige him? There he was, waiting to see the coroner's officer, and he asked for you. I said you'd probably arrive in the Kettle around eleven, but that he'd better not go there because it would be stiff with Fin's types. So he said could I get you out of there before half past.'

'Listen,' I said. 'About Ken Fiske——'

'I was telling you. Rawlings said——' She stopped. 'Is there something wrong? To do with that little rat?'

'Don't,' I said. 'Don't, Torfy. Dr. Glaisher gave him a rotten bit of news last Thursday ... I can't tell you how I feel. He must have been feeling quite frantic, and there he was, slapping my bottom and putting a brave face on. Why didn't he *tell* us?'

Torfy swung her legs off the bed, and sat there facing me, with her eyebrows meeting over her glasses. 'Tell us what?' she said slowly. 'Is he ill?'

'Leukaemia,' I told her. 'Acute, too.'

She dragged in a long breath and let it out again. 'Oh, *lord*. Poor old Ken. Who else knows about it?'

'Dr. Glaisher, maybe other people in the path. lab. The SMO probably. That's about all, I think. Neil, of course.'

'Is that what he wanted to tell you? Because you were after Ken's guts over the Emery thing?'

'Largely, yes ... Do you think we ought to tell Sally Dane?'

Torfy nodded. 'That's what I was wondering too. She's really got it bad, this time. She's been as miserable as sin ever since he went. She hasn't even tried to console herself with Johnny Winter—and she's always had a bit of a thing for him.'

'He could have told her, then.'

'Could be ...' She reached for her hairbrush and began to tidy her hair. 'Clare, I've got a problem.'

'Not one *you* can't solve?'

'Yes. Well, it's lack of information, really. If I had that I'd know what to do ... But I will *not* ask him! I've asked Jeremy, and got no change out of him, so——'

'What are you talking about?' I eased my position against

the door and stood on the other foot. I wished she would hurry up.

'Toby . . . He's asked me to the Faculty dance. Friday.'

'Well?'

'Do I go or not?'

'I see no reason why you shouldn't. What's the problem?'

'Leila Hamilton, you ass! If he's tied up with her, she won't like it, will she? But you see he asked me last year, only I'd promised Matt Affleck, so he made me swear I'd go with him this year instead. And he's just reminded me.'

I remembered what Toby had said. 'In that case it's a long-standing previous engagement, isn't it? What *can* she say?'

'Yes. But I don't want to go with a borrowed man.'

'We don't know for sure that she *is* on the scene, do we? Still, I'm working on that. I've got my spies out.'

'All right. Then I'll go.' She put the brush down and sat there looking at me in the mirror. 'Clare, remember telling me that you'd met just one man that you might have welcomed a pass from without throwing a set of jugs?'

I was wary at once. 'I don't think I put it quite like that—but yes.'

'I think I know who it was.'

That was worrying, if anything. Whatever I said there was no way of knowing how Torfy would act on it. She sometimes got carried away by her enthusiasm for sorting out other people's difficulties. 'Then keep it under your cap,' I said at length. 'You could just be horribly wrong.'

'Oh sure. I only mention it because if it *is* the man I think it is, my brother Mick knows quite a lot about his past history and what not. That's all. And it's quite interesting.'

'Bully for Mick,' I said. 'And now can I go to bed?' Had she been giving me an oblique warning, or not? But if she wanted to warn me off Neil would she have dragged me up to the court to meet him? Or wasn't she thinking of Neil at all? 'I'm practically asleep,' I complained.

'Yes, that's all. Except that—as I was saying when you shut me up—Andrews said that Rawlings and his mate picked up Ken Fiske on Saturday, around half past seven, and breathalysed him. *They* drove him back to Fin's, in a police car. And he said that "Dr. Gibbons"—presumably Jeremy Gibbon—fetched Ken's car back for him later on, and he was in yakking to the Super for a long time, and the Super said they'd to drop the charges.'

'And Jeremy never said a word,' I breathed. 'There's the trade union for you.'

Torfy smiled. 'No, not the union. That's just Jeremy. He's the biggest clam I know when he wants to be. Why, when I——'

'Goodnight, Torfy,' I said. 'Good hunting.'

The department was clear when I arrived on duty, but Sally Dane was at the CO's desk surrounded by sheets of paper. She looked as though she hadn't glanced in a mirror for hours, and she sounded harassed. 'Late supper for me tonight,' she said. 'I've got more than half today's customers to enter up before I can go.'

'But why?' I dumped my cape and went to look over her shoulder. 'What on *earth*——?'

'Everything's had to go on bits of paper since about twelve o'clock, instead of in the book. It's taken me the last hour to sort them into time-order ... Oh, the police wanted a photostat copy of something or other, and the office promised to send the book back right away. Of course, they didn't. I'm just about ready to scream.'

'They wouldn't,' I commiserated. 'But, my dear girl, why didn't you *keep* them in time-order?'

'I did, to begin with. I'm not that stupid. But then we had a mother in with three toddlers, and while I was holding one of them for the CO to look at his ears she let the other two play paperchases with this lot. She didn't even offer to pick them up off the floor! No wonder kids are so undisciplined, when their mothers set them such a fabulous example. My hat, if *I* had children to bring up, I'd damn well——'

'Shush!' I managed to get in. 'Cool it for a minute, do. Now listen, you don't need to stay. I'll do the book.'

'Hah! Sister Lamont's orders. She says you can't put yours

117

in until I've done the day ones, and I've got to get it up to date for you before I go.'

Sister Lamont, I decided, must be out of her tiny mind. '*Why* did she say you'd got to stay and do them?'

'Because I was the one who let them get mixed up, presumably. I don't know. Every blasted thing I've touched today has gone wrong. There's a jinx on me, I think. I've got my own private gremlin following me around. It's been——' She stopped and blew her nose. 'Oh, sorry. It's just been one of those weeks.' She wasn't far from tears, and I didn't like the note of hysteria in her voice.

'I'll make some tea,' I said. 'And then we'll see what's what.'

While I waited for the kettle to boil I shut myself in Sister's office, and rang through to the Home and asked for her. She must have thought it was an outside call, because when she came she said: 'Hello, this is Meerr-y Lamont.'

'Sister,' I said. 'This is Nurse Kennedy speaking.'

There was silence for a moment while she wondered why on earth I was ringing her when she was off, decided that something quite catastrophic must have happened in Casualty and braced herself to face it without flapping. Then she said: 'Yes, Nurse? What seems to be the trouble.' It was all very brisk and efficient.

'No trouble, Sister. But I found Nurse Dane here with about two hours' writing up to do, and she seems to think that you told her to stay on and finish. It didn't sound like you, so I thought I'd better check.'

'The gairr-l's mad! I told her no such thing, Nurse. I said that no new cases must go into the book until it was up to date; and that if it's not finished tonight, then tonight's casualties must go on paper.'

'That's what I assumed,' I said. 'Thank you, Sister. I'll tell her to go, then.'

'Please do, Nurse ... Eh, Nurse Kennedy——'

'Yes, Sister?'

'Is there something on Nurse Dane's *mind*, d'ye think? She's been useless this week. This afternoon I had occasion to

118

be vexed with her, and she burr-st into tears! Well?'

'I'll try to find out, Sister.'

'There'll be a man behind it, mebbe?'

'Could be,' I said. 'Goodnight, Sister.'

I made a pot of tea and carried a cup through to Sally. 'Here,' I said. 'Drink that. And then buzz off. *That's* Sister Lamont's orders, if you want to argue the toss.'

'What? But she said——'

'She said I wasn't to enter mine until the day ones were done, that's all. Nothing about your staying on. I've rung her, and that's the score. You got the wrong end of the stick.'

'Whatever did she say—ringing her in the Home?'

'Not much. Just that you must be round the bend ... When has she ever asked anyone to stay late, except to deal with emergencies? I knew damn well you'd make a mistake. So I rang her.'

She drank some of her tea, and sat back in the chair. 'I seem to have got a lot of things muddled up this week. I feel lousy, to be honest.'

She looked it. It wasn't Sally Dane to have a sliding cap on hair that hadn't been in its usual rollers for days. Or to be without mascara or lipstick. It was even more significant that she'd been biting her nails. They looked hideous, and she had always been so proud of them. After a while I said: 'Want to talk about it?'

'About what?' She didn't look at me.

I took the plunge. After all, she could only lose her temper, and she didn't seem to have the energy for that. 'It's Ken Fiske, isn't it? You might just as well tell me—it's better than bottling it up.'

She nodded. 'I suppose so ... Yes, it is. Oh, I know nobody likes him—but he's had a rotten life, one way and another. His mother went off with a GI when he was a nipper, and his father used to borrow his University grant and spend it on other women; so he had to spend all his vacs as a bus-conductor.'

'Why a bus-conductor, particularly?'

'Because it's about the best money students can get, especially if they do a lot of overtime. Unless they want to be loo-attendants: I knew one who did that, and he got about three pounds a day in tips, just for taking his own clothes brush and whisking people over. That was in a hotel, of course.' Now that she had began to talk there was no stopping her. 'Well, Ken had plenty to be bitter about ... But he was always nice to me. He spent a lot of money taking me about, too. And I know he's fond of me. That's why——' She looked straight at me for the first time, but she didn't seem to be seeing me somehow. 'You see, he hasn't written or phoned, and I don't know where he is. And—well, I thought he was serious. I was *sure* he was.'

'Did he say he'd be in touch?'

She hesitated. 'I went out with him last Friday—you know, the night I asked you about nights—and he was sort of moody that night. And on Saturday he was a bit too slewed to make much sense. But on Monday and Wednesday, before that, he was full of this new job, and he said: "When I get settled you must come to London too." So I said I had to take my State finals first—and he said there wasn't much point in that if I was going to get married ... Things like that.'

'He didn't tell you anything that was bothering him? On Friday, I mean, when you say he was moody.'

'No. He just seemed depressed, I thought. He didn't *say* anything, but he wasn't his usual self. Why?'

I didn't know whether to tell her straight or not. She wasn't, and never had been, a particular friend of mine. We had never had much time for one another. But her special buddy—a dimmish girl named Barbie Packer—had been one of the wastage statistics. She had left more than a year before after twice failing her Prelim, and we'd heard that Matron had shunted her to an SEN course somewhere in Shropshire. Most people had been hunting in couples ever since PTS, so that left Sally Dane out on a limb. She didn't have a real friend of her own. Maybe that explained a few things about her attitudes. She and Ken Fiske had quite a lot in common, when I thought about it.

'If you had to hear something fairly unpleasant,' I said,

'who would you like to tell you?'

She frowned. 'About Ken? You mean—— Is it that he's got someone else?'

'Nothing like that, no . . . Hold on, there's somebody coming up the ramp.' I went to the door. It was my Mr. Wilkins with his septic finger. 'Trouble?' I asked him.

He nodded gloomily. 'I come this morning, and that little nurse—Nurse Hughes, is it?—she didn't like the look of it. So the doctor saw it. The lady doctor. And *she* said if it wasn't no better tonight to come up again, like.'

'Right,' I said. 'Come into dressings, and we'll have a look.'

Sally put her head in as I was taking off his bandage. 'I'm staying till you tell me, Kennedy.'

'OK,' I told her. 'But you may have to wait a bit.'

She nodded and went back to her casualty book.

I had no idea who was on call, so while I soaked off the dressings I played Russian roulette with the idea. If the hand didn't need to be seen, I didn't tell her. If it did, I would ring for First On, and it proved to be Neil *he* could tell her, but if anyone else came it had to be me.

It was a mess. What had begun as a septic finger was now a septic hand. The palm and thumb were swollen and shiny, and the red streak was now a series of large blotches. I said: 'Just *what* have you been doing to it?'

'Nothing, Nurse.'

'But you must have done something! Have you had the dressing off at home?' Even Eira Hughes couldn't have bandaged it so clumsily. 'You have, haven't you?'

'Oh, well. We did take it off, yes. It was painful, see. But the missus put some ointment on it and——'

I groaned. 'Oh, Mr. Wilkins. What did I *say* to you about ointment? It was a complete waste of breath, wasn't it?'

'But it's good stuff!'

'What was it?' I asked wearily. 'What's the name of it?'

'It hasn't got no *name*. Mrs. Bellman, up College Road, she makes it up herself. Herbs and that. Did our Flo's chilblains the world o' good. Better than that old powder stuff as you put on.'

121

'That "old powder stuff" was penicillin, Mr. Wilkins. Well, you'll just have to see a doctor, I'm afraid. Sit down, will you.'

The switchboard man said: 'Yes, Nurse?'

'First On, please,' I said. 'And Thomas, don't tell me who it is. Let it be a lovely surprise—I haven't had one yet today.'

He was amused. 'Just as you say. Any details?'

'Cellulitis of hand,' I said. 'It was a septic finger yesterday, but our friend Mrs. Bellman's got at it since then.'

'Oh, *her*. Then you better *had* let them see it, Nurse.'

'Quite,' I said.

Mrs. Bellman was one of our two Casualty bugbears. The other one, popularly known as 'Mr. Mac the herbalist' went in for internal potions and female pills, while Mrs. Bellman specialised in ointments and poultices. It was a pity we weren't a profit-making concern, Sister Lamont had once remarked, because we could have paid Mrs. Bellman a lot of commission on the trade she sent us.

I looked into the CO's room. Sally was still drinking tea and staring into the middle distance. 'One of Mrs. Bellman's little triumphs,' I told her. 'First On's coming down, so shift those cups, will you. Shan't be long now.'

It wasn't Neil. It wasn't a man at all. It was Leonora Kirk who came striding in two minutes later. She was too new to know about Mrs. Bellman, so I put her in the picture before she went to Wilkins. She nodded. 'I can imagine. We had a Mrs. Fernihough, when I was at Queen's. Ought to be strung up, the lot of them. Menaces!'

She let Mr. Wilkins have a few rounds across his bows when she saw the hand, and he said: 'No need to get off your bike, Doctor! I done it for the best.'

'Well, don't blame *us* if you lose your hand!' she told him. 'There's a full report going in the book about this. I'm not going to have my nurses blamed for you and your *ointment*.' I liked that 'my'; it gave me a glow.

He said he wasn't blaming the nurses. 'No, it's just your nature, isn't it? I mean, either you got good healing flesh or you haven't.'

She snorted with fury, but her fingers were very gentle when she cleaned up the skin. 'Scalpel, Nurse. Have to make a few incisions here. He won't feel it—it's gone too far for that.'

I watched her make three neat little slits, and asked: 'Wet Eusol, Miss Kirk?'

That was what she had used last time we'd done a similar dressing together, but she said: 'No. Ointment he wants and ointment he shall ruddy well have. Mag. sulph. paste, Nurse, please.'

'Lord, *that'll* pull, won't it?' I said.

'Penicillin cream, then.'

'That's no good,' Mr. Wilkins opined. 'Penicillin, I had that on it once. That didn't do no good.'

Miss Kirk tapped the table a dozen times, silently raging. 'I think you'd better come into hospital, Mr. Wilkins. Where you'll *have* to do as you're told. You can't be trusted to leave the dressing alone, obviously, so——'

'What? Me come in here? Not likely!'

'Then you've got to promise to *leave it alone*! Otherwise we shall refuse to treat it. Understood?' She was positively bellowing.

In the end he agreed, muttering, to keep the dressing on until we'd seen it again. We put wet Eusol on it and sent him on his way. All the way down the ramp we could hear him telling us that that stuff was no good, and that it wasn't a patch on Mrs. Bellman's ointment.

While Leonora Kirk was washing her hands afterwards she said: 'Rotten business about Mr. Fiske, Nurse.'

I wasn't sure whether she knew about his illness, or whether she had heard about the Emery set-up. So I said simply: 'Yes, it is.'

'Poor devil. Dr. Glaisher only found out fortuitously, you know. Doing a straightforward blood-count for him, for this job. Tropical diseases, you know, they're always a spot fussy.'

I thought fast. If she knew—and she was a comparatively new registrar—it was on the cards that a lot of other people did too. Sally Dane could hear it from almost anyone. I beckoned her into Sister's office and closed the door. Then I put her wise. 'I'll have to tell her, won't I, Miss Kirk?'

'Don't fancy the job, do you? Like *me* to do it for you?'

Whether Torfy liked her or not, I did. She was a bit too forthright for some people, that was all. With hands as gentle as hers—big though they were— she had to have a kind heart, I told myself. 'Would you?' I said. 'It might come better from someone she isn't at all involved with. Someone authoritative. And you can talk about the prognosis better than I can. Would you *really*?'

She pushed the used towel at me. 'Try me ... Give me ten minutes with her, and then come and pick up the pieces.'

It was more like twenty minutes before I heard her go thudding down the ramp. I stole a good ounce of Sister Lamont's secret store of emergency brandy—it was in a medicine bottle labelled: *One tablespoonful every four hours*—and took it through to Sally in a medicine glass. 'Knock that back,' I told her. 'And then go straight to bed. If you go up the fire-escape you needn't see a soul. It's after ten, anyway.'

She took a fresh gauze mop from the jar to dry her eyes, and then she drank the brandy in anxious little sips. 'I'll have to go to him,' she said at last. 'I'll *have* to, Kennedy.'

'Yes,' I said. 'Of course. Somebody will swop with you. Sister'll understand.' Then I remembered that Torfy was off until Saturday, and she wouldn't want to go to the Faculty dance straight from work. And on Saturday it took me until Wednesday. That left only Luke who could cover for her, and he wasn't the sort to do it with good grace. 'Make it Saturday,' I said. 'You can have mine. I'll stand in for you.'

'But you *can't* come on, on Saturday, after doing Friday night!'

'Who can't? I can come on at ten-thirty and stay late. Whoever's on late won't mind changing.'

'That gives you less than three hours to rest.'

'So? It won't kill me. Look, Sister won't mind, I'll talk to her. You go on Saturday. Right?'

'I don't know why you're being so kind,' she said.

'Neither do I, frankly, but we all have our mad moments. Now go to bed. And try not to brood too much. Want some

124

Mogadon?'

She shook her head. 'I'm all right, now that I understand. It was not knowing what I'd done that was so horrible.'

It seemed to me that it must be even more horrible to know that Ken Fiske—if you liked that sort of thing—probably had only weeks, certainly only months, to be around, but there was no accounting for the way other people ticked. Certainly she looked a lot less fraught, even though she was blotchy with crying.

I had no more casualties at all until early morning, when there was a little spate of building site people coming for early dressings before work. It was just as well, because it took me until Meal to get the book up to date. That was when I found a telephone message that Sally Dane had scribbled out and forgotten, among the papers on the desk. It said: *Kennedy— Mr. Rogers rang. Said: "Tell Nurse K. it was first face, then back of head, then back of waist." (Hope this makes sense—it sounds like herpes!) S.D.* It did make sense. 'Back of waist' was good enough for me. I folded the note, shoved it into my pocket, and got on with the book entries. One thing at least had gone right.

When Nurse Hatherley came down to relieve me at one o'clock she said at once: 'Oh, Nurse, have you heard about poor Mr. Fiske? They say he's got leukaemia—acute too!'

I'd long since learned not to be surprised at the speed with which the grapevine assimilated facts, like an insect-eating plant gobbling up its prey, but I was curious about this one. I said: 'Now, Nurse, just how did you hear about that?'

'Oh, at Meal. At least, Nurse Hodges did, and she told me.'

Hodges, no doubt, had simply gone along with the inevitable. 'And who told her, d'you know?'

'Let's think, did she say?' Then she showed a flash of intelligence. 'Oh, what you really mean is how did it get out at all, from the residents, is it?'

'Exactly.'

'The SMO told them all at residents' dinner, Staff Soames

said. He and Mr. Sargent and Mr. Gibbon knew before, of course. Well, Mr. Gibbon knew last Thursday, they say.'

Clam certainly was the word for Jeremy, if that was true. 'Well, Mr. Affleck told Sister Duffy, and she told Staff Soames.'

'I see,' I said. 'That's how it goes, is it?' Matt Affleck always had been a gossip.

'They were wondering, at Meal, whether Nurse Dane knew. She was pretty thick with him, wasn't she? Do you think she does?'

'Of course she does. I knew too.'

'You did? But how———'

'I have my channels, too,' I told her. That would be something for her to repeat to Hodges. She would certainly think that I'd had it from Jeremy. But it was nothing to what she was going to think if she saw him pick me up on Saturday from the Home, just when the night nurses were first stirring.

I had nearly reached the dining-room before I realised that Jeremy wouldn't be picking me up on Saturday after all. I should be standing in for Sally Dane, and not off duty until after nine, and by then I should be fit for nothing but instant bed. I reminded myself to let him know. And that in the morning I must see Matron.

I had to wait until half past nine before Mrs. Corfield nodded at me and said: 'All right, Nurse, Matron can see you now.' She checked me off on her list. 'Next time, try to make an appointment, will you? I know Miss Tetlow didn't, but Miss Macintosh is finding it better. Then she can reserve the early times for the night people.'

That was yet another change in the set-up, but it should certainly cut out some of the waiting, after a night's work. Matron said: 'Good morning, Nurse Kennedy. Please note— in future I shall begin in the office at eight-fifteen, instead of nine, for the benefit of night staff by appointment. Sit down.'

Miss Tetlow never asked anyone to sit down except the more elderly of the ward sisters. I took the chair facing her and said: 'Good morning, Matron.'

She folded her hands. 'Well? You've come to prove to me that Mr. Fiske was unfit to examine Emery, I suppose?' Her voice was much harder than it had been last time and I could understand that.

'No, Matron.'

'No? You mean you can't?'

'I could, but in the circumstances I don't propose to, Matron.'

The colour flowed back into her knuckles. 'Quite,' she said. 'But there's something else?'

I nodded. 'I said I didn't believe he died of head injuries, and I think I *can* prove that, if they didn't——'

'How right you are, Nurse.'

'You know?' I said.

'But of course. Dr. Glaisher came back and concluded the post-mortem. I dare say he agreed with your diagnosis—which was?'

'Uraemia, from crushed kidneys, Matron.'

She smiled. It was the first time I had seen her smile properly, showing all her teeth. It was amazing how it lit up her face. 'Good girl!' she said. 'And what brought you to that conclusion?'

It had been a hunch, really, but I didn't think Miss Macintosh dealt in those. So I gave her the thinking that had come after the instinctive knowledge. The tutors had chewed me up too often for making what they called 'inductive leaps', and the even older generation, who made them all the time, had made it plain that it wasn't much use being blessed with a hunch mechanism unless I could rationalise plausibly afterwards. 'I'd been thinking of all the cases I'd seen with Cheyne-Stokes breathing,' I told her. 'I'd never seen it set in so quickly —not in a patient who'd been conscious—except from *damaged* kidneys, rather than straight disease. To have respirations like that from head injury he'd have had to be worse than that, or have his respiratory centre physically damaged. So I reckoned he'd had a good booting in the kidney area ... And it seemed to me that maybe they'd only looked at his head.'

'Dr. Glaisher found it, Nurse. As you'd hear if you went to

the court this morning.'

'Oh. Well, I tracked down a witness who'd seen him kicked in the back, and——'

'And you thought you ought to tell me, in case it wasn't known?' She was amused now.

'I'm sorry, Matron. It was silly of me, I suppose. But I didn't know it'd been confirmed, and I wasn't at all sure that this man would make it clear to the police. Sister Duffy rather gave me the impression that they'd just looked at the head injuries.'

'No, Nurse, it wasn't silly at all. We *might* have had an inefficient pathologist, or a careless one. It's been known! And when Sister Duffy spoke to you they *had* only looked at the head—because Dr. Glaisher was coming back to finish off. In a case where the hospital might be involved we naturally wanted the senior pathologist's opinion.'

'Of course.' I got up to go. 'Thank you, Matron.'

'One other thing, Nurse.' She took out a foolscap sheet from her top drawer. 'Sit down a moment.' She ran her eye down the sheet and then nodded. 'Yes, I thought so. You were one of the people who signed this little protest about caps, I see.'

'Yes, Matron.'

'Well, now, this is all very fine. You are perfectly entitled to put your opinions before me. But nobody has given me any *reasons*. I'm always ready to listen to a logical argument, but demands without reasons to back them up don't mean very much, do they? You all simply say you want to return to the old lawn caps—but you don't say why! I've collected a few views; now I'll have yours.'

My strongest argument had to be cut out right away, because Ken Fiske's jibe about my 'paper halo' affected only me. She wanted facts that affected all of us. 'Principally that we just don't *like* them, Matron. They feel ... cheap and nasty. *And* they cockle in the rain between the buildings, and the lawn ones dry out.'

She looked out at the mild, golden morning. 'What rain, Nurse? We haven't had any since they were issued.'

'Well, that's what people at other hospitals find.' One nurse, escorting an ambulance patient, had said so, and so had two letters in the *Nursing Times*. 'Well, we know it's supposed to be economic, laundrywise, but that's a false figure, really. Most of us have always washed and ironed our own, because——'

'Because the laundry makes a mess of them?'

'Well, yes. And we all make them up to suit our own heads, so we have to re-iron the fold anyway. And we're all willing to go on doing them ourselves, if it's a question of costs. We'd even *buy* our own, just to have them back.'

'I see. But now put yourself in *my* shoes, Nurse. I could easily *allow* your generation of nurses to do that. But then I'd be in the position of *ordering*—not allowing—new recruits to do the same. And can't you imagine the cries of "injustice" that would go up if this hospital didn't issue caps, or didn't launder them, when every other hospital did? Be fair, now. Rules have to be for everyone, not just for a privileged few, don't they?'

'It wouldn't be like that,' I said. 'Matron, surely you could tell new girls: "*Either* wear the issue disposables, *or* get and launder your own lawn." How about that?'

'Ah! But then it wouldn't be uniform, would it? There'd be six of one and half a dozen of the other.'

I still wasn't convinced. 'No. Because the new people might elect to wear disposables in PTS, but then they'd see how much nicer the others were, and they'd be only too eager to do the same as the seniors. They'd see it as a privilege.'

'Some of them, Nurse Kennedy. Only some of them. There's always a hard core of people who are lazy, or greedy, and who expect to be spoonfed.' She smiled again. 'Carry on, put your points. I told you—I'm always ready to listen to logic.'

'Then they shouldn't be nurses, Matron.'

'Ah, now you're telling me how to do my job, Nurse!' She was still smiling, but there was a dangerous flash in her large brown eyes. 'Staff recruitment is my biggest headache. If you had to decide during a brief interview—when you were trying very hard not to turn away promising material—who would turn out to be lazy or greedy, or otherwise unsuitable, do you think you'd be infallible? Because if so, you should be sitting here instead of me! If you've got the kind of antennae that can successfully read people when they're on guard, and on their best behaviour, maybe you're in the wrong job? How do you suggest we avoid the odd bloomer?'

I shook my head. 'I don't know. I'm sure every Matron has antennae to some extent, and she has time to notice things like clumsiness and bitten nails. But I suppose the only answer is to be able to give a lot more time to the selection interviews. Make a day of it, like an OCTU, so that you see them at meals, and in mixed company, and with patients. And I know you simply don't have that kind of time.'

'So? What's the answer?'

She really had me pinned down on the point. I was beginning to wish I'd never made it. 'More Assistant Matrons, I suppose.'

'Which means?'

I shrugged. 'Salmon plan of senior structure, I suppose. More sisters upgraded to number sevens. Only I don't like that, either. It's topheavy.'

'Yes. Now you begin to see that it isn't all as simple as you thought, don't you? We admin people don't just sit in our offices thinking beautiful thoughts, Nurse! Contrary to popular fallacy . . . Does administration interest you? Because if it does, come to me when you've had two years in blues, and I'll recruit you into it. All right. Run along, now. And thank you for coming to see me.'

So that was that, I thought. Emery's death wasn't going to be laid at our door after all. I had made an almighty fool of myself once more. All the same, the bit about caps had been interesting. Not that she had given us a decision, in so many words.

Torfy had gone out early. I wondered whether she had gone to court again, to see the Irishman's committal. I left a note in her room to put her in the picture about Sally Dane's going to Ken Fiske, and then I went straight to bed.

I fell asleep as soon as my head hit the pillow, I think. But not before I'd had time to think about Neil Sargent. When I closed my eyes I could still feel the tingle in my hand and arm where his fingers had touched me. I had never, all my life, experienced anything like that. Nor had anyone else ever described such a phenomenon to me. I had heard of—and known for myself—the quick little lurch of the diaphragm on seeing someone unexpectedly, someone who mattered. I'd felt—even with David Leckie, though that was alcohol-assisted—that my legs had turned to pillars of warm cottonwool, and I'd heard Torfy describe similar sensations—even, in her case, that her spinal column had suddenly become warm, quivering jelly. But that I could practically hear the crackle of static leaping between Neil's skin and my own was something completely new. New and unbearably exciting.

CHAPTER 8

AT five minutes to nine Randy had an elderly man on the couch in the CO's room. 'Watchman from the building site in Carver Street,' he explained.

It wasn't the first time, and it wouldn't be the last. 'Coshed?' I asked.

'Looks like it. The police brought him down. They've taken his statement and gone, anyway. People pinching the plumbing fittings, they said. He's not too bad. There's someone coming down in a minute—I told them to finish dinner while I cleaned it up.'

'Bit early in the night for watchman-coshing, isn't it?' I expected that kind of thing after midnight, as a rule.

'It's dark. That's all they need. They'd be more noticeable in the small hours, actually. With plenty of traffic noises, and people about the streets, nobody hears them.'

'You should have been a crook,' I said. I watched him get into his jacket ready to go. '*Why* did you go and blame your-self to the CO? After I'd——'

He dropped his working smock in the bin. Then he said: 'Tina and I thought it was right ... Anyhow, it seems to have ended without any trouble for Fin's. You heard about the case this morning?'

'No.'

'They had the committal proceedings. Oh, it'll be in Sister's paper, I expect. They charged Flaherty with murder, and he pleaded "not guilty" of course, and it'll go to the Assizes. Death was said to be a direct result of kicks to the body and head, and Dr. Glaisher said it was inevitable because both kidneys were irreparably damaged. So falls out of bed made not the slightest difference.'

'Thanks,' I said. 'Now *run*, or you'll miss your bus.'

I heard him go clattering away down the ramp, and then I went back to the patient. He was already down in the book, but not yet seen by a resident. Mr. Goldrigg, head injury from blunt instrument, 8.35 p.m. Randy had cleaned his head, and there wasn't much to see but a rising bump and a small cut. I had nothing to do but keep him company until someone came. 'It could have been a lot worse, Mr. Goldrigg,' I said. 'You were luckier than the last man. Did you see who did it?'

He nodded with his eyelids. 'I seen 'em, Nurse. Young hooligans. Whippin' me bathroom fittin's, they was. I walked into the stores hut and they jumped me.'

'Has it ever happened to you before?'

'No. Mind, only been on the job a month. Useter work for O'Connell's, the builders, labourin', till I retired.' He groaned. 'Is the doctor comin', Nurse? I feel downright 'orrible.'

One of my hunches hit me fair and square. I was pretty sure it was something I'd read in the casualty book that had begun it. And now he was feeling ''orrible' with an injury that wouldn't have felled a healthy eight-year-old.

'I'll give them another ring,' I promised. I checked the book before I did it. There it was: *William Goldrigg, aged* 57.

'You lie still and I'll find out what's happened to the doctor.'

Thomas said: 'Sorry, Nurse. There's been a bit of a hold-up. The CO's supposed to be on, but I can't find him. Miss Watts says she'll be with you in a tick. Mr. Brown did say it wasn't urgent, though.'

'It isn't,' I agreed. 'Just as long as you haven't forgotten us altogether.'

Janey Watts was down straight away, and I managed to waylay her along the ramp before she reached the hall. 'I'm not sure,' I told her, 'but I think he's lead-swinging. And I think I know why. He's acting flat out, but he isn't, and I didn't want you to over-diagnose him if it's what I think.'

'Tell me more,' she said.

'Well, it's not our business. The police are quite capable of doing their own dirty work, and——'

'Or so you've decided after Emery?'

'Something like that, yes. But he told me he'd retired from O'Connell's—and nobody retires at fifty-seven from a labouring job. Not if he's as fit as this chap is. It could just be that this is a nice little frame-up of O'Connell's to get their bathroom fittings gash. A token attack on a man they've planted?'

She frowned. 'You really think so?'

'Well, they're rather a shady firm. There was a lot of trouble about some council houses they built that weren't up to specification, and there was a lot of graft involved. One of the council architects lost his job over it.'

'How do you know these things? *I* never hear them!'

'Because we had the planning officer in as a patient, and he told us a lot of interesting little details like that. It opens your eyes.'

We walked on up to the CO's room together. 'I see,' she said. 'He's going to swear he passed out cold, and you don't think he did. So you want me to be sure?'

'Yes, that's about the size of it.'

She couldn't have examined him more thoroughly if he had been royalty. She didn't miss a single reflex, or an inch of his skin. By the time she had finished he was bored to tears. In the book she wrote: *Small occipital abrasion treated, otherwise*

133

N.A.D. Nothing abnormal detected, in other words.

I said: 'Just a butterfly plaster, Miss Watts?'

'It doesn't need that. Just a squirt of Nobecutane to seal it, that's all.' If he had fancied his chance of turning up in a police court swathed in *Journey's End*-type bandages he was going to be disappointed, I reflected.

She stayed until he had gone, just to watch. He made a great business of walking unsteadily down the ramp, but he was spry enough when it came to running for a bus outside the ambulance gate. She turned away from the window smiling. 'I think you were right,' she said. 'It would never have occurred to *me*, you know.'

'Perhaps I just naturally think the worst,' I suggested. 'Yes, what was all this about Thomas not being able to find the CO?' I opened the door for her, and followed her out. 'He's not so small that he can be mislaid, surely?'

I could have sworn that Janey hadn't been as pink as that a moment earlier—but perhaps it was just the hall lights that had that effect. 'Oh, he's somewhere about. Gone for a coffee with Matron. She does tend to trawl in the registrars after dinner now and again ... She's really rather nice, don't you think? And very intelligent.'

'Yes. A bit livelier than Miss Tetlow. But then she's twenty years younger ... Are you staying on call now?'

'Pending the CO turning up, I suppose. I hope you won't need me because I'd like to wash my hair. I had *the* scruffiest lot of minor ops to anaesthetise today.'

It was odd; we all had daily baths and washed our hair at least three times a week, in the department more assiduously than in the wards. In the wards we'd got the patients to a uniform clean state and we didn't expect to acquire dirty heads; in the department we met people in their natural state, and though most of them were pretty clean we still saw dirty heads every day, and took evasive action. Hairwashing was at any rate a very common topic, and so was the time it took from our off-duty. Yet it had never occurred to me before that the women residents had precisely the same problem: it had to be fitted in, yet they were even more constantly on call than we were, and must have found it difficult.

'I know how you feel,' I said. 'Go ahead, wash it, and I'll try not to need you.'

Half an hour later an ambulance pulled in. I wondered whether she had her hair dry yet. At the top of the ramp I stood and watched for the stretcher. For once the attendant carted their trolley in first, and then went back to help the driver with the patient. That was unusual. Either they had an extremely heavy patient, too big to be trotted up the ramp by hand, or they were a new crew, I decided. I was convinced of their unfamiliarity with Fin's when they began to trundle their patient the other way, towards the ward block instead of up to me. I called out: 'No, this way, boys!'

The driver looked back, and I saw that he was, after all, one of our regulars. 'No, Nurse. Direct upstairs, this one,' he said. 'Mr. Huxley's orders.'

That meant that it was something vitally urgent, and that they would probably be back later to give me the details for the admission slip to be made out, and the book filled in.

The telephone rang while I was waiting. It was Mother. She said: 'Have you a moment, darling?' and then said all the usual things about how was I, and was I wearing something warm under that dreadfully thin uniform dress, and when she'd gone through all the routine she said: 'Oh, I *really* rang to give you a message from Father, darling. He was so pleased to see you the other day, but he thought you looked tired.'

'What was the message?' I reminded her.

'Oh, yes. The message. Well, I don't know what it *means*, Clare, but I dare say you will. He said you'd know, anyhow. He said I was to tell you he'd seen Dr. Hamilton, and the answer was yes, but it's a secret until next week, and the name is Gibbon.'

'Gibbon?' I echoed. I felt winded for a moment. 'Mother, are you quite *sure* he said Gibbon?'

'Quite sure, darling, because I know it made me think of those ivory castles.'

'*What* ivory castles?' She was getting worse, I decided.

'Well, teeth. You know. Only that's actually Gibbs, isn't it?

135

But it's *like* Gibbon, if you see what I mean. I said to myself:
"If I think of ivory castles, I'll remember," and I did.'

I didn't know what she was talking about, but then I often
didn't. She had a butterfly mind, but she usually got names
right, through some strange mnemonic system of her own
which seemed to involve attaching groups of ideas to TV
commercials. And if ivory castles made her think of Jeremy
Gibbon, then Jeremy Gibbon it was. 'Thanks,' I said. 'Why
didn't he ring me himself? Then I'd have *known* it was right!'

'Well, darling, I thought *I'd* like to speak to you. Are you
busy? Lots of casualties and things?'

'Thousands,' I said. 'Can't you hear the terrible din they're
making? I'd better go, before they tear the place to pieces.
Tell Father I like his new houseman, by the way.'

'Has he got *another* new one? Oh, dear. Just as he gets used
to them they seem to go. Why doesn't he find one he can stick
to?'

'Mother, they *have* to move on. They can't stay as juniors
all their lives!'

'I thought they just grew up into registrars.'

'Not without different experience,' I said.

'Oh. Well, it wouldn't do for me. I like continuity.' She
paused for a second to blow her nose. 'Such a cold again,' she
said. 'Your father always says it's my allergy, but I know it
isn't. I tell him, I know I'm not a doctor, but permit me to
know when I've caught cold ... As I was saying, I like continuity. If I had to keep changing my daily women I'd go
mad.'

'Yes,' I said. 'Well, take care of yourself. You know my
prescription—lots of hot onion soup. Nice to hear you.'

'Goodnight, darling. Be good.'

'I'll try,' I said.

When I got back to the CO's room the ambulance was pulling out. I put a small tick on the next line in the book, to
remind me to leave a space for the entry when I did get the
particulars. It was all very irregular, but emergencies often
are.

Hodges came to relieve me, for the second time. What was even more unexpected was that she came early, to send me to First Meal. People who are relieved normally have to wait for the third sitting. I said: 'What's wrong? Doesn't your junior like me any more? Or are you dieting?'

'Both,' she said. 'Ruined her night, you did, knowing all about poor old Ken Fiske before she told you. She thought she was on a winner there ... If it isn't a rude question, who *did* tell you?'

'It's a rude question,' I said. It seemed a pity not to give her a little mystery to think out when she enjoyed them so much. 'And how come I get to surgical seniors' Meal for a change?'

'Well, I thought you might like it. And Sister Duffy doesn't really mind when we relieve you, so long as we do, does she?'

'I wouldn't know. I never see her, down here. Touch wood. So you can't tell me what the food is, not having sampled it, can you? A fat lot of use *you* are as a relief.'

'Let's hope it's a nice surprise, then.'

Most of the surgical seniors were at First Meal, with the medical juniors. That was so that the surgical juniors could run across the bridge to their oppo on the medical side if they needed senior advice, instead of having to go up or down a floor. It only applied to extreme emergencies, like pulmonary embolisms and cardiac arrest, when there was no time to telephone but only to run halfway across the bridge and yell. By the same rule the medical juniors would have the surgical seniors within yelling distance during Second Meal.

I sat among the surgical lot, and we talked about caps, after I'd reported my conversation with Matron, and her little spiel about admin difficulties. One of them said: 'What could she do to us if we simply *wore* our old ones? And said nothing?'

'She'd say it wasn't uniform,' I told her. 'But I'm game to try it on, personally. In fact I've been considering it ever since the disposable ones were issued.' That wasn't strictly true: I'd been thinking about it ever since Ken Fiske had said his piece in the office that night. I could forgive him now for practically everything else, but that still rankled. An ordinary halo wouldn't have been so bad, but a paper one sounded pretty cheap, as if even the priggishness he accused me of was a fake. 'Has anyone else handed them in to the sewing room? I haven't. They'll only throw them away, and it's a waste. We might need them in another hospital, so I kept mine.'

So, it seemed, had everyone else. By the time we got to the chocolate mousse we had agreed that next night we would all arrive on duty wearing the most beautiful confections we could produce, with a fold like a knife-edge and every gather in place.

Before I went back to the department I asked: 'Any of you taken in an emergency? Because I haven't had the details yet.'

'It won't have been medical,' Staff Soames said. She looked down the table at the juniors huddling together to chatter. 'Any of you people had an admission?' she asked them.

They nearly all shook their heads. One of them said: 'Wasn't there one that went straight to theatre, Staff? I thought I heard a trolley in the lift.'

'First I've heard of it.' Soames looked round the other seniors. 'None of you had anything?' She turned back to me. 'Well, there you are. Must have been a ghost. I certainly haven't had anything into Intensive.'

'There *was* a patient,' I said. 'Dobson was the driver. I *spoke* to him.' Then I thought of something else. 'Could it have been a sick resident, gone straight to his quarters?'

'That's a thought,' Soames said. What had the ambulance driver said? I tried to remember. She had the same idea. 'Did they *say* they were going to theatre?'

'No, I don't think so. "Straight up", or something like that. And it was Mr. Huxley's orders.'

'Perhaps the SSO's cartilage has gone again. He ought to have it done, but he won't.'

It was the first I'd heard of that, but Soames had gone on ahead before I could say so.

I stopped in the hall to have a word with Thomas in the switchboard office. 'Solve a mystery for me,' I said. 'You know what goes on. Finger on the pulse and all that. Somebody's hiding something.'

He took off his headset, and looked at me. 'What kind of

138

thing, Nurse?' He turned to flip out a couple of cords as the flaps came down.

'Well, it's all very mysterious, isn't it? First you can't find the CO. Then somebody's brought in on a stretcher, and doesn't apparently go to the medical side, or the surgical side, or Intensive, or theatre. Or maybe he did go to theatre. Could it be that we've a sick resident? If not, it doesn't add up, does it? I'm not given to seeing things, and I *saw* that case arrive.'

'Well, like you say, Nurse, it does sound a bit funny. Perhaps——' Thomas's expression changed, and he turned back to his board and flicked his key across. It didn't fool me, because I'd worked the thing, but it would be good enough to fool Sister Duffy if she was standing behind me, and that was what his face had said.

'Nurse Kennedy! I don't send you a relief nurse to let you come and waste time gossiping with the night porter, do I?'

I turned round as slowly as I dared. It had to happen, of course: there, just disappearing round the bend of the corridor, was Neil Sargent's unmistakable back. Now he could add porters to his little list of residents and policemen. But would he? Hadn't we shaken hands on a new deal? 'No, Sister,' I said meekly. 'I'm just on my way back.'

'Then get a move on,' she told me. 'All the others have gone back to their wards. You *would* be the last to leave the dining-room.'

I didn't tell her that I'd also been the last to arrive there. It wasn't worth it. I said: 'Sorry, Sister.' Then I went.

At the low point of the ramp I peered up through the glass roof at the theatre on that side. The lights were certainly on, but not the big operating lamp. Some of the others went out as I watched. So they *had* been working. It could, of course, have been a sudden ward emergency that wasn't an admission. That would account for the trolley in the lift as well. But it still didn't explain the ambulance and the stretcher I'd seen—unless Soames's idea about the SSO had been correct. At any rate, it hadn't been Neil. I'd just seen him. I stopped worrying about it, now that I was sure of that.

He was standing in Sister's office, talking to Hodges when I went in. Standing over at the window, with his back to the room, as he so often did. 'So the disappearing CO is back in circulation,' I said. 'Thomas made it sound as though you'd vanished into thin air.'

'He would,' he said. Hodges made a face and rolled her eyes, meaning that he was in an odd mood and I'd better watch my step.

'Lamb stew and chocolate mousse,' I told her, as she walked out. Then I looked at Neil again. 'Janey Watts had a better idea. She said you were probably having coffee with Matron. Were you?'

He shook his head, and turned to face me. 'No. Talking of coffee, Clare, let's break a few rules for once.'

'You're the doctor,' I said. 'Such as?'

'Such as your making coffee for both of us.' He tried to smile but somehow it didn't quite come off.

'With pleasure.' Obviously there was one rule for him and quite another for Jeremy and the policemen. That really wasn't very logical. 'Do we use Sister's best cups, or the issue ones?'

'Just the issue will do.'

I switched on the kettle and fetched the milk from the blood frige, and when I had made the coffee he sat in Sister's chair and I took the one opposite. He was staring into his cup the way he'd done in the Cherry Tree. Something was difficult to say, that was obvious. As gently as I could I said: 'Neil, what's wrong?'

He drank some of his coffee before he looked at me. 'Why do you say that?'

'You look the way I felt when I thought I'd have to tell Sally Dane about Ken Fiske.'

'And did you tell her?'

'No, Miss Kirk did. Well, everyone seemed to know, and it would have been rotten if she'd heard it just casually on the grapevine. I'd got as far as asking her who'd she choose to give her bad news, if she had to have some, but——'

'What a funny question. People can't choose their informants very often ... What about you? Would *you* have a choice of messengers?'

'Oh, a man,' I said straight away. 'Somebody kind; somebody I could cry on. You can't cry on women.' Then I looked at his face again. It was all there, only I didn't know what it was. 'You mean I might want to cry on you? What is it? Tell me, for God's sake. Don't just sit there like the angel of death!'

'Not that bad, Clare. But it could have been.'

'Is it *Torfy*?' I knew that everyone else who mattered to me was all right.

He shook his head. 'Clare, I was missing earlier because I had to go out to a consultation with Mr. Huxley. You know his registrar's on a long weekend; and now that he's getting on a bit he likes to have a younger man with him, to reinforce his opinion, as it were.'

I frowned. 'Yes?'

'They say doctors make bad patients, don't they?' He got up and went back to his station by the window, half turned to look down into the dark ambulance park. 'This one had let it go too long, too. He, of all people, ought to have known better —but they never do ... The *very* worst strangulated hernia I've ever seen. He was terribly shocked. I didn't think ...'

I was slowed-up, bewildered. 'I'll get there in the end, Neil. It must be the night-duty mind-block syndrome, I expect. You went to a p.p. of Mr. Huxley's, and brought him back for op. Is that it?'

'Yes. And Sister Duffy put the fear of God into all the surgical seniors, and sent Hodges to get you to their meal. All briefed not to tell you a blind thing.'

Then it did hit me. Hard. I stood up and went to him. 'Neil? Neil, *could* it be my father? Only I don't see——'

He gripped my elbows. 'Yes. It's all right. I *think* it's all right. But it was a damn near squeak.'

I got a firm hold of the lapels of his white coat and hung on tightly. 'But Mother *rang* me while that ambulance was here. She gave me a message from him.'

'All part of the strategy to keep you out of it.' His mouth

141

was unsteady. 'We didn't want you to be worried and upset until we knew where we stood.'

I was still thinking of Mother. 'She can't *do* things like that, Neil. She couldn't keep a secret to save her life, especially when she was scared stiff. And she must have been.'

'Couldn't she? But she did, didn't she?'

It didn't seem possible. 'When can I see him?' I had never admired Mother before. Loved, but not admired. 'Where is he?'

'Not yet. He's in Intensive.' I remembered Soames, at Meal, giving nothing away at all. 'Sister Vivian's looking after him herself. He's very shocked, as I told you. But he's getting packed cells, and everything else we can give him. And I'm going to stay up. All right?'

I did cry on him then. He held me close to him while I did it, and I must have drenched the front of his silk shirt. I kept my cheek against it for a little while after I'd dried my eyes because it felt warm and safe. I knew then exactly what Professor Morris meant about the reassuring heartbeat. When I stood up straight again I said: 'Sorry. But maybe I needed to do that.'

'I know. Now sit down and drink the rest of that coffee.'

While I did that I thought things over, and realised what a tremendous put-up job it had been. The ambulance that didn't wait; Hodges, briefed not to say anything, instead of Hatherley who could keep nothing to herself; the surgical seniors, all in on it and chattering about caps to keep me occupied; the one medical junior who had been too observant; Soames, with her apocryphal story about the SSO's cartilage. 'The whole darn hospital,' I said. 'They were all in it. How *kind*. Even Sister Duffy, chalking me off when I was trying to pump Thomas ... I thought it was *you*, you see.'

'My dear Clare, if doctors and nurses can't be kind, then who can? They're supposed to be professionals at it.'

'But to do all that for *me*. It's incredible.'

'You'd have done the same for Sally Dane ... It was for your father too. He couldn't say much, but he did say one thing. "Don't frighten Clare." And he's a VIP, after all. We

142

do as he says. You see, there's some advantage in being a Prof's daughter, even if you used not to think so!'

'Poor Father,' I said. 'And *I* know why he let it go on too long. He's never had a single anaesthetic in his life, and it's his one secret fear. I suppose that's funny, isn't it?'

'Yes,' he said soberly. 'It's funny. Later on, when he's out of the wood, I'll remind you and we'll laugh.'

'Please God,' I said. 'But there's Mother! We can't leave her in the house alone, waiting for news. Somebody must——'

'She isn't, and she wasn't. She rang you from the SSO's room as soon as Huxley got her here in his car.'

'She's *here*?'

'At the moment she's resting in one of the mothers' rooms in Children's. You'll see her in the morning.'

'But the Children's people were at Meal, and—— You mean Sister had been over and told them, too?'

'No, I did. I rang them ... Clare, I want to go back to Intensive. You'll be all right, won't you?'

'Yes. But if anything goes wrong ... you'll come yourself, won't you? If you can.'

'I promise.'

I stood at the top of the ramp and watched him walk away with his long quiet strides, and looked at the point of hair at the back of his neck and wished I could reach out and touch it. It would have comforted me very much to do that.

CHAPTER 9

IT must have been nearly seven o'clock when Sister Duffy came tramping along the hall. For some reason best known to herself she was whistling. I had never heard her do such a thing before, nor had I ever imagined anyone at her level whistling a Beatles tune. She came to stand at the office door stone-faced as ever, for all the whistling, and I think that was when I realised that she didn't know how forbidding she looked, that it was her natural neutral expression and not a face she put on to scare people. 'All right, Nurse. Don't get up,' she said. I stood up just the same, out of habit. 'I only whistled to show you there was nothing wrong. I came to say the CO's on his way down. He said if you saw him first you'd think it was bad news. He wouldn't ring, for the same reason. Right?' Then she went.

Neil came a minute later. 'He's pulled up wonderfully,' he told me. 'You can peep at him when you go off, but don't let him know you're there. His blood-pressure's climbing beauti- fully. The old boy's basically as strong as an ox, or he wouldn't be here at all after last night.'

'Thank God,' I said. 'Oh, Neil, you look *so* tired.' Then I began to laugh, though there was really nothing to laugh at. I suppose it was relief. 'You need a shave. You look like Richard Burton being a survivor from something.'

He felt his chin. 'So I do. I'd better go and get one.' He went on looking at me intently, as though his mind was photo- graphing me for the last time. 'No, I won't. I'll borrow the Minor Ops razor. There's something I want to do before I go back to breakfast.'

'But it's a cut-throat!'

'That's what I always use. The only way to get a decent shave. I can see your education's been neglected.'

I fetched him a clean towel from the stock cupboard—a new soft one that Sister Lamont hadn't yet issued for use, and sat in the middle of the hall to wait for him.

When he came back he said: '*Now* will I do?'

He was beautifully smooth, and some of his colour had come back. 'Much better,' I said. 'But you looked more interesting when you were being Burton ... Will you do for *what*, any- way?'

He was so close to me that I couldn't have lifted a hand between us to test his chin for myself, when he said: 'You

144

can't tell by just looking.' Then his arms went round me. 'Oh, Clare,' he said. 'Will I do for this? Please!'

There are things that are quite impossible to describe in ordinary words on ordinary paper. I would need a way of communicating with lights, jewels, colours and scents, and with harmonic arrangements of electronic impulses, with fur and velvet and spices, and somewhere the heady tang of Harris tweed, to convey what it was like to be kissed by Neil Sargent in the middle of Casualty waiting hall at half past seven on a golden October morning. Other people were able to describe it to me. Staff Weaver, Jessie Blake and Randy, who all walked in on it, said—or Jessie did and the others agreed—'There were practically shooting stars circling round your heads.' I said that our heads were not all, and that personally I'd been sure they could see little red arrows all over me like the ones in the circulation diagram hanging on the wall in the schoolroom.

Neil went away soon after they arrived, and as I followed him I heard Jessie Blake say: 'Who's been using my razor? Young Lochinvar, I'll be bound.' And Cathy, sounding troubled, said: 'I hope to God he's serious. She'll break her shy little heart if he isn't.' It was interesting to know how others saw me. Torfy had always told me I was shy, but Torfy said a lot of things. If Cathy Weaver said it too, maybe that was what had been the trouble all along, not Ted Gaunt, or David Leckie, or anyone else. It had been me, all the time. I took a deep breath of the hazy morning air, and the lavender morning light, and knew that I could never again be shy where Neil was concerned. Not after a kiss like that. It had felt like a surrender for life, and that was the way I wanted it to be.

I peeped at Father before I went over to dinner. Sister Duffy would just have to understand if I made myself late. He didn't look nearly as bad as I'd feared he might, though he was very grey and still. Sister Vivian was still there, and Charge Nurse Howitt had come on early, just because he had the Professor of Surgery in his ward. Little Mr. Hasan, the senior of the two Intensive HSs, was hovering too. It made me feel very humble and grateful, and I tried to say so, but it came out

145

rather damply.

Sister Vivian said: 'He'll do, Nurse. And I'll stay on nights while he's critical, and then he can come over to me in S-seven. Don't you worry. I don't allow any backsliding in my ward, as you well know! Nor does Mr. Huxley. You can see him again before night breakfast.'

'Thank you, Sister,' I said. 'If he *had* to be ill, then I'd as soon you nursed him as anyone I know.'

She looked pleased. 'After all you suffered at my hands during your training?'

'*Because* of it,' I explained. 'I learned more from you than from any other sister in the place. You're the best nurse of the lot, and we all know it. I'm glad he's with you.'

'Oh, what a tarradiddle!' she said. Her face was pink, in spite of the tired puffiness round her eyes. 'Now listen, Nurse, your mother was awake until five, and she's sleeping now, so don't disturb her. She sent you her love. You just get off to your dinner now, and go to bed.'

She must have repeated what I'd said to all the others in the sisters' sitting-room, because even Jeremy knew about it when he came down to Casualty that night. 'Buttering up Sister Vivian now,' he said. 'Who isn't a tactician?'

'Not tactics, truth,' I told him. 'She's a tartar, but she's a great nurse. She puts the patients first *all* the time—not the establishment, or the staff, or the service, or anything else. If she didn't get what she wanted for her patients she'd go and shoot the Group Secretary personally. Or the Regional Chairman ... Anyhow, what sort of tactics is it for you to invite me out on Saturday? I can't come, though, because I'm standing in for Dane so that she can go and see Ken Fiske. Sorry.'

'Damn *good* tactics,' he said. 'One way and another it's the last chance I'll ever get to take you anywhere, ducky. After this week, no can do.'

'I know,' I told him. 'My voices told me. Congratulations, Jeremy.'

'You're the very first. Thank you very much. As a matter of fact I don't think you could have come, quite apart from that, if our CO's in his right mind. According to him none of us are

146

allowed even to speak to you, much less take you out on the spree, from now on. Or am I telling tales out of school?'

'You are,' I said. 'You've been here longer than any of the others, and you must know that anything discussed in the residents' dining-room is sacred, and not to be repeated to the dear nurses. Isn't that the unwritten rule?'

'True. Only this wasn't *in* the dining-room, ducky.'

'Where was it, then?' I had visions of myself being discussed across the table in theatre.

'At the bedside of your revered parent, not half an hour ago. He's making great strides, I must say.'

Father had been sleeping when I'd looked in myself. 'It was? He surely didn't say all that in front of *Father*?'

'Oh yes. He was sort of asking permission, as you might say, and dragged me in to vouch for him. Very proper too. I like to see these things handled in a civilised manner, I must say. I told your papa he need have no fear, he could safely hand you over.'

I began to laugh. 'I like your nerve! *I* haven't been asked whether I want to be handed over.'

'No, ducky. But you will be. Just as soon as I get back to the common-room and report that you're in a receptive frame of mind, and not surrounded by hordes of casualties.' He warded off the blue pack of cottonwool I threw at him. 'Careful! If I go back marked that'll be the CO's keep-off signal. It's the bringers of evil news who get massacred, not——'

'I'll damn well massacre you myself in a minute,' Neil said at my elbow. 'For Pete's sake go and patrol the gynae ward or something, and leave my girl alone, you great oaf.'

When Jeremy had gone skipping off down the ramp I said shakily: 'Your girl, Neil?'

'If you'll have me. Will you?' He led me into Sister's office and lifted my cap off very carefully. 'How pretty that is. So much nicer than those paper things. Much more feminine.' It was a pity, I thought, that Matron couldn't hear that. He set it down on the desk as delicately as he might have touched a woman in eclampsia, where a feather's weight might set off a fatal convulsion. Or a tetanus patient. Then he turned back to

147

me and held out both arms in a safe, harbour-shaped curve.

That kiss might have gone on all night if the ambulance siren hadn't penetrated it. As it howled in the park below us he handed me my cap and said: 'There's so much to say, my love. We'll never have time in this place. But I'll be saying it with everything I do until I can talk to you again.' He smiled. 'Don't be surprised if my sutures come out as embroidery saying *Neil loves Clare.*'

It took me a long time to tell Torfy next morning while she laid up Dr. Martin's allergy clinic. I didn't let her get a word in about the dance. 'And what *about* his past history?' I asked her finally.

She frowned. 'Whose?'

'Neil's, of course. You said that Mick——'

'Oh, *that*. I didn't mean Neil, I meant Jeremy. I thought that was the person you reckoned to feel so safe with. You said you never saw him; well, you never went out with Jeremy, so——'

'Jeremy is well and truly booked,' I said.

'He is?'

I remembered then. 'I'm *so* sorry, Torfy, I forgot. I was so worried about Father that night that it went out of my head. Look, it's a secret until next week, so all I can say is that Leila Hamilton's *not* hooked up with Toby. Only with his chum. That's what he must have been telling Dr. Monahan, and I got the wrong end of the stick.'

Torfy walked silently across to the end of the room and performed four cartwheels in a row. Then she hugged me. 'Dear girl, how *did* you find out?' She picked up her cap and rammed it on again. Somehow it sat in the right place.

'I didn't. Father did. He pumped Dr. Hamilton.'

'Bless him. Then he deserves to get well quickly. Not that he'll dare to do anything else with Sister Vivian on his back.'

'And how *did* the dance go?' I asked at last.

Torfy positively smirked. 'I don't really know. We spent most of the time sitting in Toby's car, talking in riddles for *hours*. I did sort of gather that either he wasn't interested in Leila or he's the best actor at Fin's.' She sat in the revolving chair and whirled herself round at speed. 'I think I'll settle, this time.'

'Yes,' I said, 'I think I will too.'

She looked at me. 'Hey, you're wearing an old cap! I don't know how you dare.'

'I dare,' I said. 'You don't think I'd allow myself to be proposed to in a paper one, do you? I have my pride.'

'But you didn't know that he——'

'I can dream, can't I? This one happened to come true, that's all ... Oh, hell! I'd forgotten. I've got to come back on duty at half past ten, to stand in for Dane.'

'You're crazy.'

'Look, I promised. Because of her going to London. And I forgot to see Sister about it, too.'

'I don't *care* what you promised. You're not coming on duty today, here or anywhere else. Tomorrow, if you like. Not today. You're going to bed, my girl.'

'But Sister——'

'It's Sister's weekend. Weaver's in charge. And I can stay late, if that's what you intended to do.'

I really was too tired to argue. 'All right, Torfy.'

'Buzz off, then. Give my love to your father. And your mother.'

'I will. But Mother's gone home now, so he must be better, I think. And I haven't even seen her, poor lamb. She was asleep when I went up yesterday. But her sister's with her at home—you remember Auntie Jo?—so she'll be all right. I won't ring her in case she thinks it's Intensive panicking.'

'Will you *go*? Cathy Weaver isn't on until half past eight, but I'll explain. You come on tomorrow, when you've had a good sleep and calmed down a bit.'

Father was sleeping again, but he looked a good deal more like himself, and they'd stopped the drip and cleared away some of the paraphernalia. Sister Vivian said: 'He said I was to wake him if you came up, but I'm blowed if I'm going to. I know what he wanted to tell you, anyway.'

'Do you? What, Sister?'

'Well, he said: "She'd better tell that young man of hers not to take so long about it as Leila Hamilton's did." Does that make sense?'

'Oh yes, that makes sense, Sister. You can tell him he needn't worry about that, because I don't think he's half as patient as—as Leila Hamilton's young man!'

'I see.' For a responsible ward sister of forty-plus she managed to look almost mischievous. 'And do you know who that is, Nurse Kennedy? Since you seem to have such good radar.'

'No comment, Sister. I gather it's a secret until next week. Unless you worm it out of Father, of course.'

'Maybe I will. Shall I be surprised?'

I had once heard her remark that Jeremy was a born bachelor. 'Our Mr. Gibbon isn't the marrying kind,' she had said. 'He's totally committed to registrarism.'

'Yes, I think you may be *very* surprised, Sister,' I said. 'It shook me, certainly.' I left her wondering.

It seemed odd not to be going on duty again that night. I went down to late supper, so as to have it with Torfy. She didn't come off until after half past nine, and when she did come she looked terribly scruffy. 'I know,' she said. 'Don't tell me. I look as if I'd been dragged through a hedge backwards, as Sister Lamont would say. If it's any comfort to you, that's the way I feel too.'

'Busy?' I reached for the salad cream, salt and pepper, and ranged them in front of her plate. 'Who's on tonight?'

'Luke Martin, and you know how slow he is. I couldn't leave him with fifteen old dears all with facial cuts, could I?'

'How come? An outing or something?'

'No. They were all at a Darby and Joan Bingo session. You know—free tickets, and all the prizes donated. Blankets and coal vouchers and such. Good by stealth, as it were. Apparently the Co-op hall has a glass roof, and some young idiots thought it'd be a great jest to climb up there and smash the lot. Of course they looked *up* instead of keeping their heads down —really, you'd think people who'd gone through air-raids would have more sense, wouldn't you?—so they all got cuts ... Oh, I nearly forgot.' She fumbled in her side pocket. '*Billet-doux* for you.'

I took the envelope. 'From whom?'

'No idea. It was on the blotter in Sister's office. One of your many admirers, no doubt.'

I ripped it open quickly. 'Yes, I've got a date.'

'Tonight?'

I nodded. 'Quarter past ten.'

'That's going it a bit, isn't it?'

'Some people don't come off call until ten,' I mentioned. 'And if he's done all those stitching jobs in Cas he'll want to snatch a bath first, I dare say, before he steps out.'

Torfy grinned. 'I'm seeing mine briefly at ten, and to judge from his voice on the phone it could be a pretty vital interview. Just so that we don't coincide, like two couples at the same end of an empty beach, where are *you* to wait?'

'Nowhere you'd choose,' I assured her. 'I imagine yours will be in the grounds?'

'Where else? It's as undisturbed as anywhere.'

'Well, mine isn't, so we shan't intrude.'

I was at the OP gate, where Neil had twice dropped me and said goodnight, just before a quarter past. His car was there already, with the engine running. I'd had time to think something out properly as I walked across the ambulance park, and I must have been smiling about it when I got into the car, because he said: 'Penny for them, Clare.'

'Later,' I told him. 'It'll keep ... Father's a lot better, isn't he?'

'He's being a model patient, according to Sister Vivian.'

'High praise,' I said. 'She's not easy to please, is she?'

'No, indeed.'

'I've never thanked you for all you did that night, Neil. I couldn't have stood it without you.'

'You could. One adapts oneself. Parkinson's law—the courage expands to fill the necessary space, or whatever.'

I was talking nothings, and feeling more than I could

express, and I wondered if he was doing the same. He was driving slowly round and round the block as though he hadn't made up his mind where to go. I said: 'Where are we going, Neil?'

'Nowhere, really. Anywhere that's quiet.'

'There's always the park,' I suggested.

'But the gates are locked at this hour.'

'Only the car gates. The little wicket's left open, for pedestrians.'

He considered it. 'No. On second thoughts I know that if we go walking in the park at this juncture I shan't let you come back until dawn. Or I shall steal you away altogether, and you'll never be seen again, like little whatsaname.'

'Little who?' I said.

'You know. The little girl the fairies stole.'

'Oh, in *Up the Airy Mountain?* I can't remember her name, either ... Well, the Cherry Tree's open till midnight. They don't have many people in, because they double the prices of coffee after eight o'clock to keep out the *hoi-polloi*.'

'Damn the Cherry Tree,' he said. 'I'm stopping right here.' He switched off the engine and pulled on the handbrake.

Right here was exactly outside the French window at the end of the Home. And the window belonged to the sitting-room of Matron's flat, which had its own outside entrance on the garden side. But that didn't seem to matter as he turned in his seat to face me.

He didn't touch me at first. 'Clare,' he said, 'I love you so much. I have ever since the Rag ball. Only you weren't ready then. There was something you had to grow out of, wasn't there? Has it gone now?'

'I threw it away last night,' I said. 'At least, I burned it, with my paper halo. I think after all it was only a sort of shyness. Only I'm not shy with you.'

He held out his arms then, and kissed me. Only not quickly like that. Not *passé historique*—he kissed me, and that was that; but the imperfect—he was kissing me, he continued to kiss me—is what I really mean. English is sometimes an inadequate language. It was even more shattering than it had been the first time, in OP hall, when he had shaved in Minor Ops specially. I was sure that if I were to extend a finger towards any of the metal parts of the car a great blue spark would jump the gap.

After a while he said lazily: 'Clare, what *were* you grinning about when you came across the ambulance park?'

'Only that I really ought to have seen the point when you said I'd been talking to Jeremy for twenty minutes on Sunday night. I must have been a bit dim.'

'What point, my love? That I was jealous? I suppose I was.'

'No, not that. That you couldn't possibly have known what time Jeremy left the department unless you'd met him on the ramp, *on your way down there*. He could have come from anywhere if you'd met him beyond the autoclave room. So *you* must have——'

'*Touché.*' He laughed. 'Yes, you're right. I wanted to come down and begin all over again. And then I met him, right on the corner, and I had to pretend I was looking for him. I'd no other valid reason for being there, as far as he knew.'

The light went on in Matron's sitting-room. We watched her walk across to the sideboard. The SMO, Dr. Stillwell, closed the door and went to stand with his back to the fireplace. She turned to offer him one of the glasses she was carrying, and then she came to the window and drew the curtains, but looking back at him over her shoulder. 'Well, well,' Neil said. 'So that's the way the wind blows? I knew he had concert tickets, and he made no end of palaver about getting Jim Kane to stand in for him, but I'd no idea who was going with him. The things that go on!'

'She looked frightfully slim in that long dress,' I said. 'She's a very attractive woman.'

'All the confirmed bachelors are suddenly seeing the light at the same time,' Neil said.

'Including you, darling?'

'Me? I saw it a year ago. Otherwise I'd never have come to Fin's as CO.'

I sat bolt upright, to look at him properly. I could just see

153

his eyes and his mouth in the fringe of light from the Home porch lamp thirty yards away. 'That's absurd. It can't have been as important as that. Not then.'

'It was. I was all set to apply for a pretty minor consultancy —in Sheffield, of all places—and then Mick Bates said: 'The CO's job's going at Fin's, if you're still thinking about Torfy's little chum.' I'd talked to him about you, off and on ... Well, I applied and got turned down. It went to a man named Worcester, from Guy's. I'd made up my mind that if I was to have you I'd get the job, and if I wasn't I shouldn't. You know how one does?'

'I know,' I said. 'I did that over telling Sally Dane. If you came down, you had to tell her; if someone else came, I had to do it myself.'

'But you didn't.'

'No, because Leonora Kirk took it out of my hands. You know what she *is*. And I was glad to let her ... Go on, about the job.'

He shifted his arm behind my head and began to stroke my hair with his other hand. 'Your hair fairly crackles,' he said.

'I know. I crackle all over when I'm near you. It was fantastic the first time it happened. My arm ached for hours.'

'When was that?'

'The day we went to the Cherry Tree.'

'Yes. That was when I first felt it, and I knew that things were coming right, at last. That you weren't afraid any more ... Well, there I was, telling myself that the job wasn't for me and neither were you, and going round like a bear with a sore head. You ask Mick Bates some time. Because I didn't want to go to Sheffield one bit. So I applied for an SSO's job in London—it made sense at the time. And then they telephoned me and said that Worcester was down with typhoid ... You don't know how happy that made me. And then that first night I lost my temper with Fiske, and took it out on you, and I was sure I'd ruined everything. And I got it into my head that Gibbon was chasing you ... You see, I'd thought about you long enough to have become pretty possessive.'

I smiled. 'Jeremy says you've warned them all off.'

'Wait till I see him! Not that he's any room to talk, with his own engagement being announced next week.' He bent his head. '*What* were you muttering into my shirt?'

'I said let's beat him to it.'

'Exactly what I feel. Snubs to him, as we said at my prep school. When we go in?'

'Yes,' I agreed. 'Because I'll have to tell Torfy.'

'We'll tell everybody, my love.'

'Only we can't really, not until——'

'Quiet,' he said. 'That's all been taken care of. If you'll just remove your mistrustful little head from my breast pocket for a second—thank you. Now, close your eyes until I tell you to open them.'

I kept them closed obediently, even when I felt the cold metal sliding on to my finger. Then I felt him reach up, and heard the click of the interior light going on. 'Now,' he said. 'And I do hope it'll do.'

It was a lovely ring. An enormous fire-opal framed with tiny diamonds. 'Neil! How *did* you know? It's the most beautiful opal I've ever seen. Look at the light in it!' I said.

'Well, I consulted the only people I could think of—Torfy and your mother. They both said you were zany about opals.'

'They have a magic of their own,' I said. 'So have moonstones. I'd have settled for a moonstone, darling. You didn't have to spend your all ... But it fits, too. How did you manage that?'

'Put it down to a good surgeon's eye, and plenty of opportunity to look at your hands. I knew it wouldn't be very far out, and if it's right that's a pure fluke.'

'You're *very* clever,' I told him. 'And *very* generous. And I love you so much I feel I'm going to fly apart into little pieces, like a Mills bomb.'

'Please,' he said. 'I'm supposed to be off duty. I've mended enough people for one day. And if we're going to break the news tonight it's time we began, isn't it? I don't think we'll begin with the SMO and Matron. I've been called a good many things, but never a spoilsport.' He dropped a quick kiss on my ring, and another on the end of my nose. 'Off you go, before I get involved again.'

Torfy's light was out, but I didn't care. She couldn't be asleep if she'd just come in from meeting Toby. I went in and flicked it on again. She peered at me over the sheet. 'Lord, I was sure it was Home Sister galloping about. I wasn't asleep.' She sat up. 'I put the light out to keep an eye on you two idiots out there. Right outside Matron's flat—you must be dotty!' She was grinning like a turnip lantern, and she looked dotty herself without her glasses. 'What *do* you think?'

'What do you?' I said.

Our left hands shot out simultaneously. Hers was an emerald, rose-cut, not one of those deadly square ones that people seem to like so much, in an antique setting. It was nearly as nice as my own.

It must have been well after one o'clock when we finished drinking the tea she made, and went to bed. In the morning I should be able to tell the others in Casualty. On Monday afternoon there would be Sister Lamont—if she didn't hear earlier.

When I did tell Sister Lamont she said: 'So that's what happens when you go on night-duty! And I suppose the ring's round your neck on a piece of NHS bandage, just like everyone else? Well, go on, show it to me, gairr-l!'

I pulled it out between my front buttons and let her look at it. 'Some people think they're unlucky,' I said. 'I don't.'

'That's *bonny*,' she told me. 'Unlucky? Here I've just brought your registration certificate over for you. And haven't I just heard that Mr. Sargent's to take over when Mr. Huxley retires in the new year? Unlucky, indeed!'

I stared at her. 'You've heard *what*? Sister, you can't mean it!'

'Och, he'll not have told you yet. It was only known this noon. Mind you know nothing when he tells you, then, or——'

'Or what, Sister?' I tucked my ring away again.

'Or I'll not come to your wedding, Nurse Kennedy!'

'We can't have that,' I said. 'So I won't know until he tells me.'

'Good,' she said. 'Now, would you mind going and getting on with Mr. Huxley's outpatients? They're getting out of control across there ... Besides, the CO's still his temporary registrar.'

I flew across the hall. Horace had nearly all the cards out ready for me. I said: 'Bless you, Horace. Remind me to show you something before I go.'

'Just as you say, Nurse. I've sent the first two stars in to get ready. And Mr. Huxley isn't here yet, nor anyone else.' He glanced up at the big wall clock. 'They won't be long.'

'They'd better not,' I said.

Sister walked across the hall to speak to me. 'Oh, one thing, Nurse. Staff Nurse, I mean. Matron says that in future all staff nurses may wear the old lawn caps.'

I bent my head to show her. 'I've been wearing mine since Friday, Sister.'

'Make the most of it, my girl,' Neil said behind her. 'If you're going to get any wear out of them you'll need to sport three at once ... Good afternoon, Sister Lamont.'

She widened her eyes in reproof. 'Good afternoon, Mr. Sargent. I'll thank you not to waste my nurses' time in idle gossip.' Her mouth twitched at one corner. 'Och, you're a terrible man! But you'll make a fine consultant, I don't doubt.'

As she sailed away I said: 'What *does* she mean?'

'Later,' he told me. 'Send in the first two non-stars, please, Nurse Kennedy.'

'Yes,' I said obediently. 'Sir!'

I was as cumbered about as Martha for the next three hours but it was worth it. Every time I passed Neil's desk on my way to Mr. Huxley's room I could look at the back of his neck. I could imagine the rest until we were both off duty again.

When Mr. Huxley was leaving he looked out at the window and said: 'Dear me, Nurse, it's pouring with rain. What a pity—it was such a lovely month.'

Neil and I looked at one another and laughed. As far as we

157

were concerned it still was. I said: 'Raining, sir? Is it? I hadn't even noticed.'

'Nor had I, sir,' Neil declared.

Mr. Huxley shook his head over us. ' "Ah me, what eyes hath love put in my head," ' he said. 'No, don't see me out, my boy. I'm sure you've better things to do.'

We had.

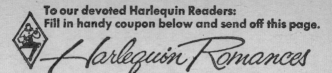

To our devoted Harlequin Readers:
Fill in handy coupon below and send off this page.

Harlequin Romances

TITLES STILL IN PRINT

〰〰〰〰〰〰〰〰〰〰〰〰〰〰〰

Harlequin Books, Dept. Z

Simon & Schuster, Inc., 11 West 39th St.
New York, N.Y. 10018

☐ **Please send me information about Harlequin Romance Subscribers Club.**

Send me titles checked above. I enclose .50 per copy plus .25 per book for postage and handling.

Name ....

Address ....

City .... State .... Zip ....